Sharon Breeling is a Colorado girl. She lived in the Rocky Mountains for many years before settling in the Denver area. The mountains are her backyard, and she hikes and fishes there. Last summer, she climbed her first fourteener. Sharon started writing short children's stories as a hobby and decided to write a novel. Traveling to small towns and getting to know the people there provides inspiration and characters for her books.

This book is dedicated to Michael Breeling. He shared so much of his life with me and inspired me. He is a dusty old cowboy at heart. Thank you, Mike, for being a part of my life and for believing in me and letting me tell some of your story.

Sharon Breeling

THE WINTER'S TRAIL

AUSTIN MACAULEY PUBLISHERS™

LONDON • CAMBRIDGE • NEW YORK • SHARJAH

Ordering Information:
Quantity sales: special discounts are available on quantity purchases by corporations, associations, and others. For details, contact the publisher at the address below.

Publisher's Cataloging-in-Publication data
Breeling, Sharon
The Winter's Trail

ISBN 9781643789101 (Paperback)
ISBN 9781643789118 (Hardback)
ISBN 9781645365587 (ePub e-book)

Library of Congress Control Number: 2019915833

The main category of the book — FICTION / Sagas

www.austinmacauley.com/us

First Published (2019)
Austin Macauley Publishers LLC
40 Wall Street, 28th Floor
New York, NY 10005
USA

mail-usa@austinmacauley.com
+1 (646) 5125767

I would like to acknowledge the town and people of Calhan, Colorado.

Synopsis
Winter's Trail

The Ironwood Ranch sat several miles southeast of Calhan Colorado. It boasted wonderful grass for cattle, canyons or "hoodoos" to get lost in and a fantastic view of Pikes Peak especially at sunset. David grew up on this ranch. His father was a rancher and a woodworker. The ranch was full of his handcrafted furniture and mantles, and the gate was a sight to behold. His mother was a beautiful woman who understood the loneliness of an only child and strived to entertain and instill values in her red-haired, lanky son. The day David's father bought him his first horse began a life-long friendship of three unforgettable horses, the horse trainer Juaquin, and a love for the ranch like he had never known. The strong young man served his country in Viet Nam and, thanks to his mother, started writing in his pocket notebooks thoughts and events that documented his life and his strong feelings about the love of his life.

Ruth came into his life to complete it, but slipped away until his deep love for her brought her back from the death's door and back to the ranch. The whole town and most of the surrounding county came to know and care for this extraordinary man and shared in his life's journey.

Chapter 1

Rosie was waiting out by the big front porch for David. He was up very early to saddle her up and feed her before he got ready for his ride. From the weight of the saddle, the horse knew it was a ride along the fences. The rides lasted several days and before leaving, Rosie knew if she left the barn and wandered over to the sprawling ranch house, there would be some homegrown carrots waiting for her. Ruth had a big garden full of carrots for the horses. She and David didn't eat them and they grew big and sweet. Nothing else grew in that garden and the neighbors joked about it, but it made her feel good to grow them for the horses.

David tried to not wake his sleeping wife. He turned on the bathroom light so he could get his other boots and stopped to look at his wife. Her long blonde hair was on the pillow and her hands were in little fists under her face. No matter how quiet he was, he always managed to wake her. She rolled over, smiled at him, stretched, and asked him not to leave without a cup of coffee and something for breakfast. He nodded, gathered his things, went to the big open kitchen, and sat down at the old wooden table. His father had made that table out of an old cottonwood tree that had been struck by lightning.

David was about seven and remembered his father showing him how to use the woodworking tools. It took a while to finish it. He thought about his mother and how proud she was of that old table and how she took out the big can of paste wax. David and his mother spent hours putting a soft finish on the wood. It's still beautiful. The tools were long gone, but David still had the wooden box that they came in. He had spent many happy hours at that table: meals, homework, play, and just talking.

While Ruth was putting coffee on the stove and starting some steak and eggs, her husband was putting on his boots. They weren't his usual worn working boots. They were his nice boots, handmade in Raton, New Mexico. They were hand tooled green leather on the top and soft brown cowhide on the bottom. They were handstitched and tooled and were the finest cowboy boots he had ever seen. Through the years, he had worn them to parties, dances, funerals, and church. When he put them on, they fit like a glove and felt like slippers on his tired feet. Ruth was puzzled about the boot choice, but she shrugged her shoulders because she knew his work boots needed to be resoled again and it required a trip to Colorado Springs and waiting for several days.

David put his work boots in the corner by the door. He opened it and told Rosie he would be right out and sat down for some strong coffee and breakfast. Ruth made nice breakfasts since her retirement from being a teacher years ago, and she never let him leave without one. David finished his breakfast and Ruth picked up his plate. As she walked away, he admired her tight jeans tucked into her worn Ropers and old University of Colorado sweatshirt. She wasn't always this fit. She had gotten ill and lost weight but she still was pretty to him.

That blonde hair would not go up into her signature ponytail till she left to do her chores. It was very pretty and was still tousled from bed. She wore no makeup, yet her still smooth and unwrinkled skin was pink from sleep. She was most beautiful in the morning. David had more gray in his brown hair these days and his handsome face was now getting weatherworn. He stood up to go and finish getting ready but before he left the room, he went to the sink full of suds that his wife had her hands in and stroked her hair and kissed her neck. And just so she knew it was really him, tickled her side till she giggled. That giggle was gold. He loved it every time.

In the bedroom, he reached onto the closet shelf, took down his Stetson, opened the top drawer of his dresser, and grabbed his spurs. They weren't just any spurs. They were nickel silver with rounded rowels, not sharp ones and were made by Crockett. They were trophy spurs that he won in a rodeo. The old western wear store in Fountain put them up as a prize and he valued them more than any cash he won. He wore them when he went to the rodeo or out to a dance. He hadn't worn them in a very long time. That old store went out of business a while back, times have changed. He sat in the chair, fastened them on, and grabbed his spiral notebook and a number two pencil to put into the pocket of his nice, white western shirt. The little notebook had a spiral on the top and the pages were lined. The pencil was new, so he snapped it in half so it would fit in his pocket. Ruth asked him why he had on a white shirt today and his response was that he was going to have a long talk with God today and give thanks. He wanted to look his best. She laughed. Everything he did was for a reason and she was always surprised with his explanations.

David hung his sweat-stained Resistol hat on the hook above his work boots by the door. He had had that hat a long time. It had been stepped on by a bull, been rained and snowed on, and had been reshaped more times than he could count. It was a silver belly 10x beaver hat and was a light grayish tan color. It was soft and fit his head so well that a wind couldn't take it off of him. But today was special. He put on his black Stetson 10x beaver hat. It had a simple horsehair band on it. On went his holster with the second-generation Colt peacemaker. It was his father's gun and he learned to shoot it at a young age. It had a six-inch barrel in a .45 long colt caliber. David was a good shot, but it helped that he had a gun he could count on. He also carried a Winchester model 94 30-30 caliber in his saddle. The wood was worn on it, but it always hit its mark and saved David's life more than once.

He opened the kitchen door and stepped out on the porch. Rosie was in a hurry this morning and his three-year-old border collie, Pete, was running circles around her. It was cool out on the porch. The sun was just starting to come up and the eastern sky was a slight orange color. Ruth came out with full cups and sat on a rocker next to his to have one last minute with him. She packed food, a thermos, and water for him and he was ready to go. David called the dog over to his chair and made him lie down. Pete was too hyper to take with him. The last time the dog went with him, he got tangled up with a skunk and wasn't allowed in the house for a week. Besides, Ruth needed someone to talk to. The couple enjoyed a little more time and a cup of coffee together before he got up to mount and ride. Ruth liked to sit close, touch his arm, and savor the smell of strong coffee and Old Spice. He got up and wrapped his arms around his wife, kissed her soft neck, and threw his leg onto his horse. As usual, before he left, Ruth reminded him that if he got an ATV, the job could be done in less than a day instead of two. The sixty-seven-year-old man just laughed and said it would be called riding, not ranching then. Besides, the machines frightened the calves and made them impossible to handle.

He pointed Rosie east towards the pretty sunrise and set out to fix the fences. Tumbleweeds were hard on fences and this year saw record amounts of weeds. As David headed towards the ridge and the east fences, he turned Rosie around. The sun was up enough that he could clearly see the big red barn and the long, low, wooden farmhouse with the huge porch.

He could see the rockers and even Pete on the porch, but where was Ruth? Then he saw her come out of the house and step down off the porch to the yard. Her blonde hair was in a ponytail and she was ready for chores. She stepped out into the driveway and the rising sun reflected off of her golden hair as she waved at him. He raised his hand to wave but decided to blow her a kiss. Then he turned the big red horse around and they disappeared over the ridge. The Ironwood Ranch was southeast of Calhan Colorado. It was the biggest one in El Paso County and had a view of Pikes Peak from the hill.

Chapter 2

David sat tall on his saddle. It was a high-backed Hamley Saddle, plain with no silver or tooling on it, with the exception of the small silver plate on the back of the seat that said, "Hamley Saddle Company, Pendleton Oregon." It was custom-made for David and fit him well. He could ride for days. Rosie just got her new annual saddle pad and blanket and was comfortable too.

He didn't want to miss a thing about this sunrise. The air was crisp and cool and there was still a smell of sage in the air even though it was late in the fall. A few tumbleweeds rolled past him as he left the yard and went over the first ridge and past the big cottonwood trees and stock tank. The grass was thick here and Old Dan was the only horse at the tank this morning. David stopped to hand a couple of his wife's giant homegrown carrots to the horse. As he reached out to pat the old horse's forehead, Old Dan raised his tired head up to meet the rancher's hand. Their friendship went back many years and there was nothing they wouldn't do for each other.

David finished feeding Old Dan the carrots and made a clicking sound so Rosie would move. They rode through the cottonwoods, past the old burned-out stump of the very large old tree that was brought down by lightning.

He remembered, he was about seven and the crash woke him up from a sound sleep. Early the next morning, he took the pickup out with his father to cut that old tree up. His father was very careful to measure the wood and cut the trunk and branches into uniform lengths. David's dad was also a woodworker. He spent lots of hours making this fallen tree into a table that saw many meals and lots of homework and long evenings of reading or playing a boardgame with his very patient mother. There wasn't much time for games or fun on the Ironwood Ranch, but his mother always set aside time for him to be a boy.

His chores gave David plenty of time to be alone with his thoughts. He learned to ride at an early age and worked the cattle with his dad and other cowboys. As he rode past the loading chutes and corals, he remembered the days of hard work. There were the calves to separate and brand, and the steers to weigh and send to the auctions. David liked working at the auctions. But most of his chores were close to home. He brushed and cleaned the horses and cleaned out the barn. As soon as he was ten, Dad taught him to drive a loader so he could move hay into the barn. The woodcutting built up his muscles and he was glad when the house was converted to gas. But his all-time favorite chore was to help his mom feed the chickens and collect the eggs with her. He didn't even mind cleaning the chickencoop or gardening with Mom. She would sing, tell jokes, and ask him about the books he read, school, and his friends. David had two good friends since the first grade. Jake and Christopher rode the bus with him. They were rough-and-tumble ranch kids with large families and were like brothers to him. Sometimes they would ride their horses over to the Ironwood Ranch, swim in the stock tank, practice calf roping, and even play a little football in the dirt yard. That scared the chickens and there wouldn't be eggs for a few days, but his mother never scolded him for it. The sound of the boy's laughter made her smile.

There were no chickens now. David really didn't like them and got his eggs and chicken at the neighboring ranches.

His mother encouraged him to join football and rodeo while he was in school. She wanted him to not miss out on fun with his friends just to work on the ranch. She never missed a game; he could see her in the small bleachers. It was a small school, all in one building and the team was made up of kids from surrounding towns, some all the way from Kiowa. Farm kids played good football. His friend Jake went to college on a football scholarship. David wasn't as good a player, but his mom cheered in the stands and he could still hear her voice today. She went to rodeo events, but they made her nervous. He didn't hear her cheer then. She sat in the grandstands, way at the top by the announcer's booth. Sometimes he thought he saw her cover her eyes. She never complained though. His dad used to rodeo and while they were out working, he would show him calf roping tricks and how to handle his horse. He never wanted David to ride a bull, though. He said that something gets into a bull when there was a rider. He used to say it's as close as you can get to the devil. His dad had a few scars and broken bones, and as he got older, those bones hurt.

David had made a promise to his mom that while he was in school, he wouldn't ride a bronc nor a bull. He had other skills. He got his first quarter horse when he was a teen. Rusty was red and not too tall. He had one white foot and couldn't stand still.

One Saturday when David was fifteen, his dad took him to the auction in town. It was a special one. They had quarter horses, saddles, tack and King ropes, boots, and hats. He was only going to get a new hat but as he and his dad were walking around looking at the horses and tack, this horse surprised him. The Four Sixes Ranch in Texas brought five big trailers with five horses each. They were big, shiny, new trailers and as they walked each horse off, David started to daydream about having his own. There were horses on the ranch but none like this. He knew he could rope a calf and do just about anything at the rodeo with one of these beauties. His dad watched him walk around and listen to the men examine and comment on each horse. For a little bit, he lost sight of his teenager in the crowd of men and horses. Then all of a sudden, he watched David fly through the air as if someone pushed him really hard. The boy got up and brushed himself off and before he could take a step, a short red horse came out of the crowd and pushed him again. People stopped to watch the match between the boy and the horse and started to laugh. It seemed like the horse won when David turned around and confronted Rusty. His face was angry and for every step he took forward, the horse would back up a step. If he turned his back, Rusty would push him again. Finally, David extended his hand and the horse nuzzled it with its nose. Later, the father and son were sitting in the stands at the auction.

David liked to watch livestock auctions. All of the Four Sixes horses went for top dollar and went fast. The last one to go into the arena was Rusty, the short red horse with one white hoof.

The boy was startled when his father put in the first bid. Then he waited and waited. No matter how much the auctioneer talked, no one wanted to bid against his dad. The horse was his. The rest of the time was spent getting tack and, of course, his hat. David's hat was too small. He rarely wore it and with his red hair and freckles, he came home with a lot of sunburns. So, he got his Resistol working cowboy hat and felt really good. They had not planned on buying a horse when they went to the auction that morning. A quarter horse was a luxury on a working ranch. All their friends came to congratulate the boy on his horse as he held his reins and waited for his dad to come with a trailer. One was loaned to him by his friend, the county sheriff. He didn't buy a horse because he thought the boy should have one. David carefully loaded the horse in the trailer and as he did, his father and the sheriff were chuckling. They couldn't tell where the teenager's hair ended and Rusty's hair began. Those two belonged together and the whole town could see that they were going to win a lot in the rodeo circuit and would be the best of friends. It didn't happen often, but these two bonded in front of the whole town. Everyone was just as proud as if he was their child.

It was hard to drive home without looking out the back window of the old Ford pickup at the trailer with Rusty calmly looking back. After the third time, his dad told him to calm down and relax, they would get the horse home safe. David sat back down in the seat and stared at his dad for a very long time. What would make a frugal rancher spend that money on a horse? He thought long and hard about his father's character. He was a very kind man who was firm and fair with his only child. He expected the boy to do chores and carry his weight but wanted the stars for him too. He would have long talks with David and always told him to dream big but not forget where he comes from. He admired his father that day. Not for buying him a horse, but for the respect the others at the auction showed him. He had a reputation in Calhan, sat on the grange, and was a member of the town council. He didn't talk a lot, but when he did, he was listened to. His dad had been a rancher all his life and knew cattle. He gardened and grew the most beautiful hay in the county. Most people in town called him "the carpenter" because his woodworking was so beautiful. He built the ranch house they live in with his own hands when the two-room house became too small for the family. His furniture was all handmade and if you had a chair or table he made, you had a work of art.

David just stared at his dad all the way home from the auction. He was the most amazing man he had ever known.

The next day was Sunday. David's mom took him to church that morning and his dad stayed home to do the chores. David wanted to stay home and help, but his mom said his education comes from many places and that day is a beautiful day to give thanks. His friends were there and were again congratulating him on his horse. Jake offered to come over later and help him saddle the horse and start working with him. After church, they went home. Mom was making fried chicken and a cake. Normally, David would stand over her waiting for his favorite meal. He volunteered to mash potatoes and shuck corn every Sunday if it meant having fried chicken any faster. But as they turned into the driveway, he could see Rusty in the corral behind the barn. David changed his clothes and ran to see his new friend. Rusty heard him running and ran towards the fence. It seemed to take all day to get a bridle on that horse. Every time the boy walked forward, the horse would inch backwards. It almost seemed like a game and Rusty was the winner. But when his mom called to him that dinner was ready, David gave up and took the bridle to put it away. As he walked away, Rusty would get behind him and give him a little push. David caught on and soon was ignoring the horse. Keeping his back to the horse, he walked around the corral twice until Rusty nudged his arm with the bridle in it. David slipped it onto him and then climbed over the fence and ran in for dinner.

Not even a funny new horse could keep him from enjoying Sunday fried chicken.

After the showdown in the corral, Rusty was fun to saddle and finally ride. It was on his terms and each day, they had to play the game, but it got easier every day.

Soon they were practicing for the rodeo. David's dad would help him and his friends would come over. Roping calves came easy for David, he had been working cattle with his dad and the ranch hands since he was old enough to sit in the saddle by himself. Along with getting toys for Christmas, he would get a practice calf or ropes. And many times, his mother would go out to practice with him and would take pictures of her five-year-old roping the calf dummy. Rusty thought it was a big game to play and he was good at it. Sometimes he was so intuitive that David didn't have to touch the reins or tap him with his foot. It was quite a sight to see the red-haired teen on an equally red-haired horse. The friendship between them was growing. Rodeo season was coming, everyone was getting ready. Rusty was more ready than anyone else. He seemed to be a little bored and managed to play jokes on his red-haired friend. Sometimes, he would wait till David was relaxed and stop short just to roll him off of his back. His latest thing was to stop short and back up. If David gave him a little kick, he would walk sideways. The poor boy would get off in frustration and end the day. The saddle would come off and Rusty would be brushed, watered, fed, and then let out into the corral by himself. After a while, the horse noticed that if he played pranks on David, he wouldn't get treats. Sometimes, there were carrots or apples from the trees behind the bunkhouse or extra feed. He got extra on days he cooperated and quickly learned to do well for extra treats.

As the weather got warmer, David liked to go for a little run on Rusty. And Rusty really liked to run. One day, they were out for a good gallop and went down towards the small canyon on the ranch. It was long, narrow, and looked like the badlands. The colors were beautiful inside the canyon. David didn't spend much time in there, his dad said the colored rock was like chalk that would crumble and was dangerous. That day was a sunny day that he and Rusty ended up at the mouth of the canyon. David tied the horse to a bush and went in on foot. He wouldn't want to hurt his horse, but he wanted to snoop around the little canyon. As he was walking in and out of the colorful spires and caves, a little wind came up and David did not hear the rattlesnake that was sunning himself around the corner. When the boy saw the snake, it was too late. He jumped back in fear and the rock beneath him crumbled. He fell between the rock wall and the rattler. He didn't have room to stand as the rock formation jutted out over his head, and he had no choice but to scoot on his backside further in the crevasse to get away from the snake. But this time, the snake was agitated and was coiled and rattling loud. David was stuck. Just when he thought he would have to take a bite in order to escape, he heard horse's hooves on the rock. Around the corner came Rusty, raised up on his hind legs with a terrible angry look on his face. He snorted and stomped right on the snake's head. He kept raising up and stomping until David stood up. Then he finally stopped and backed up so to let the trapped boy out. David led him out of the canyon and rode him home. He called out to his father as soon as he saw him coming out of the barn. When they got there, David was too upset to tell his dad what had happened. His father was alarmed and took the boys hat off, dipped it into the stock tank and poured the cold water on his head and face. David calmed down and told his father what happened. Together, they went over every square inch on Rusty and didn't find any sign of a bite. The next day, David's dad rode to the canyon and brought home the rattle. That was all that was left of that snake. He showed David how to dry it out and wanted him to keep it. It would always remind the boy of Rusty's loyalty, and he never forgot the horse saved his life.

Chapter 3

It was Memorial Day weekend and the first rodeo at the fairgrounds was going to be today. David went very early that Saturday morning with both his parents. Rusty and his dad's horse were in the trailer behind the old Ford. The saddles and tack were stowed in the bed of the truck and the three of them were squished in the seat of the cab. David had grown so much that summer that his broad muscular shoulders made no room for his mom between them. She didn't mind. Soon, he would be driving the old truck and she wouldn't have this closeness with him again. He smelled good today. Fresh soap and Old Spice like his dad. It would be a different smell when they got home. David's mom would take her binoculars to the grandstands and sit at the very top like she always did. His dad would saddle his horse and take him out to the arena and ride him around to warm up. His rodeo days were over when he got married, but he worked the events as the pickup man. He would herd livestock out of the arena and offer a short ride to the bronc rider who managed to stay on the full eight seconds.

David and his dad saddled their horses and seemed to talk to everyone in town. The first events would be starting in about an hour, and his mother opened the thermos of hot coffee and broke out the bacon and egg sandwiches she made that morning. They were tightly wrapped in foil and warm towel and were still hot when they chowed down. The bread was homemade and toasted. They each had a couple of sandwiches and coffee and were ready to go to the arena. They liked to get there early so they could warm the horses up in the arena. Everyone who knew about Rusty was very anxious to see him perform. It was all everyone in the stands could talk about. The calf roping was early that morning and everyone in town watched David and Rusty. When it was his turn, the grandstands got strangely quiet. The gate opened and it was as if Rusty was flying. His red mane and tail flew in the air and he kept pace with the calf. There was nowhere for the calf to go and the roping was done in what seemed like record time. David roped the calf, dallied off the rope on his saddle horn, and jumped off his horse. Now, without a rider, it was up to Rusty to keep the rope tense. He slowly backed up to take up the slack and keep the rope taut. David grabbed the calf and threw him to the ground in one easy motion. Out came the pigging string and three feet were tied together. He jumped in the air and threw up his hands to show he was done. The whole time, Rusty held the rope taut. The clocked stopped at 9.2 seconds.

At first, there was a loud roar from the grandstands and then more silence. The score was posted and another loud cheer. David had won first place. He took off his hat, rubbed his horse's nose, and the two of them left the arena. The applause was deafening. Rusty held his head very high. He was a natural.

The boy took his horse to the trailer and removed the saddle, gave him a quick brush and some of his mother's prize carrots that he snuck inside his jacket. A big crowd had gathered to see the horse that won and pet him, so he tied him up and returned to help his dad and watch the bull riding.

David loved the bull riding. He stood at the rail with his friends with one foot on the bottom rail and waved his hat at the riders who went eight seconds. Eight seconds was a lifetime when you are on a bull. A couple of his friends were allowed to ride, but he had promised his mom. All he could do was watch and try to understand all of the twists and turns and study the big muscular creatures. Today, there were only two that stayed on for the full eight seconds. David liked to imagine himself on the bull. Not now, but someday.

After all of the events, he fed and watered the horses and helped his dad to put them in the trailer for the ride home. Then it was a bath and dress up in his favorite white shirt, string tie with the turquoise slide his dad made from a stone he found on the ranch after a summer rain. He put on his black Justin boots and his best Wrangler jeans. He sat down for dinner with his mom and dad, they were dressed up too. Cold fried chicken and potato salad was dinner tonight. They were all going to the dance at the grange. David's friends pulled up outside and honked, and he grabbed a chicken leg and ran out the door. With a casual wave, he rode off in his friend's old Chevy sedan.

There was an old cowboy band at the grange that night. David and his high school buddies were standing around the punch bowl and tipping their hats to the high school girls on the other side of the room. No one was brave enough to ask the girls to dance, but it was fun to just hang around and talk about the day. He got a lot of congratulations, but the boys spent a lot of time talking about Satan. The best ride on that bull so far was 6.5 seconds and a lot of cowboys got banged up. The band was playing now and "Walking After Midnight" by Patsy Cline started to play. The teen boys hushed up as David's dad and mom started to do a pretty two-step across the floor. His mom had a nice skirt that twirled and everyone noticed how smooth and in touch with each other's moves they were. They only looked at each other with a smile as they danced. A couple of times around the floor and more couples started to join them. Soon the floor was full of dancers, but no one danced like his mom and dad. It made David smile. He was shy but did manage to stumble to the other side of the room to ask a girl to dance. He was very grateful his mom pushed the big kitchen table aside and spent hours teaching the boy to dance. He felt awkward but managed to get around the dance floor with the girl. He liked this girl; she was in most of his classes and had red hair too.

When the dance was done, he went back to his buddies. The talk was still about his rodeo performance with Rusty and that bull Satan. The rider that day didn't make it more than 3 feet out of the chute before he was tossed off. Luckily, he jumped that day and made it to the fence and over before the bull caught up with him. There was a lot of joking and daring. Someday, one of them would get to ride Satan, but not David, and not that day nor any time soon. He promised. The boys ducked out of the dance early and piled into their cars. Cruising town here wasn't discouraged. After all, the main road through town was less than ten blocks long. Soon, they would tire and head home.

The rest of the summer was filled with ranching, rodeo, and dances. David got his driver's license. His mom took him out in the old Ford pickup and spent three hours with white knuckles, teaching him the clutch and how to shift. When it looked like he finally caught on, she drove home and handed him the keys. She told him to drive all over the ranch but not to go past the gate. He went to the corral and took Rusty out, threw some carrots in the back, and drove off with the horse chasing him. It made his mom laugh. That boy didn't go far without the faithful red horse. She hoped he would always feel this way.

Fourth of July rodeo came. The family drove in and parked. They were next to a new Chevy pickup that was the nicest colors; turquoise and white. It had lots of chrome and a big V8 engine. All the guys stood around it and admired it. David only made some money from the rodeos and he managed to spend it on evenings cruising town with his friends. That day, David won first place in his event. He won a little cash and a beautiful pair of nickel silver spurs. He wore them on his work boots and they made a nice sound when he walked. They reminded him how much he loved to rodeo. When the day was done, he took Rusty over to the trailer to go home. His friends had special plans for that night. As he got closer to the trailer, he noticed it was hooked up to the new Chevy. When he wandered around to the front, he saw his dad and asked him what was going on. His dad showed him his shiny new keys and said that was his new truck. He ordered it from the dealership all the way in Denver and they delivered it to the fairgrounds. Then he reached into his pocket and took out the old Ford keys. He handed them to David and said the rules are on the front seat. The old Ford was all his. It was a pea green and had rust on the rear fenders. It had a dent in the right front fender where it was hit by a bull. He refused to go into the pens and took it out on the truck. The rear bumper had seen too many days of hauling horse trailers but it would see more. David loved that truck. He went home, cleaned up, called all of his friends, and with a chicken leg in his mouth and one in his hand, ran out to the truck to go get his friends. They would be so surprised.

The rest of the summer was spent on rodeo, helping his dad, and spending time with his high school buddies. One evening, just before school started again, David and his friends were cruising the tiny town. They would drive from the cemetery at one end to the auction grounds at the other; it was starting to get old. One of his friends said, "Let's go to Curley's." Curley's was the old brick building by the co-op. It was a bar and served up a good hamburger once in a while. It was packed on rodeo weekends, but other times was a quiet place the locals went to for a cold one and to dance to the music on the Wurlitzer jukebox in the corner. The underage boys were allowed in as long as they bought a pitcher of Pepsi and a burger. They couldn't stay past eleven and Curley watched them like a hawk to make sure they didn't drink. Curley was the owner and his buddy Chet was the one-armed bartender.

The boys walked in and sat at the table closest to the bar. None of them had been in here before. If they ate burgers in town, it was at the sale barn and sometimes had a hotdog at the gas station. The town was very small. There were really no restaurants because mostly everyone lived at the ranches and cooked at home. That night, the boys had rodeo money and decided to eat at Curley's. After their eyes adjusted to the dim lights, they could see the bar and dance floor. There were tables in a circle so the two-step could be done in the middle. The bar was old varnished wood with a brass bar along the bottom so cowboy boots could rest on it. There was about a dozen bar stools and Chet stood behind the bar, wiping it with a damp bar towel. There was a large mirror on the wall behind him that reflected the light that got to it through the bottles of liquor on shelves in front. The beer taps dispensed Miller, Coors, and Budweiser. The boys ordered a pitcher of Pepsi and four glasses. They all ordered a burger with cheese and sat looking around nervously. There were two couples dancing to an old Hank Williams song and three guys were sitting at the bar nursing a cold beer. No one seemed to care that the boys were in there, but they all knew the boys' names and their parents.

Curley was a gruff man in his sixties. He wore a dirty apron and sat at the end of the bar, drinking strong coffee out of a mug that must have been white at one time but was now coffee-stained. Curley had written "Hands off, Curley's cup" in bright yellow paint on the cup, and no matter how many times it was washed, you could still see it. Chet served the boys the soda and stood and chatted with them for a bit. He was a handsome man at one time. Dark, thick hair and a signature pencil-thin mustache. But now he had a scar above his left eye and was missing an arm. He had a deep voice and everyone liked to hear him talk. He was in the navy in San Diego and had gotten drunk one too many times. One night, he drove onto the base drunk and had an accident. He woke up a week later missing his arm. His girlfriend left him and the navy made him leave. His story about how he met Curley changed every time he told it, but they had been friends since he left the navy. He was already in his forties that time and was the bartender. He could do a lot with just one arm. He washed dishes and bar glasses, and even swept up at the end of the night. He held the broom under what remained of his severed arm and pushed it with his good hand. He was as good as any man with two arms. Neither man would tell anyone why they ended up in this tiny town. Everyone thought they arrived on the Rock Island line and never left. The burgers were ready and David and his friends were amazed that with a little shuffling, Chet could carry all four to the table and set them all down in the right place.

It was getting late and everyone went home. David and his friends had stayed around a while to listen to music and hear the stories from Curley and Chet. It was close to midnight when Donna came in. She was Curley's wife and came to count the money and take her husband home. She smoked a lot and had the gravelliest voice of any woman they had ever known. She washed Curley's cup and stood behind the bar counting the money. When she was done, she turned off the lights and shooed the boys towards the door. As they were leaving, Chet asked them to come back. He liked these fresh young cowboys; he had a million stories to tell them. They all went outside and got into their cars. Chet walked the block to his house, but Donna and Curley got into an old tan Cadillac and drove off over the tracks. David and his friends went home and decided that Curley's would be their occasional hangout. They wanted to hear more about Chet and Curley.

The rest of the summer flew by and even after school started, the boys would go hangout in the bar. This was their last year in school, they were seniors and had plans to make. There was a war going on and college to think about. It would be a busy year of dances, football, and evenings in town. David's parents didn't mind him hanging out, but he needed to be home early on school nights and he never stayed when the weather was bad. David only went out on weekends; he had to help his dad with the ranch chores and he never missed a chance to ride Rusty. Sometimes if he was out late, Rusty would be waiting by the porch for him. No one knew how he escaped the corral, but he was noisy and would wake the boy's parents so David had to watch the clock. Rusty won David a lot of rodeo prizes those two years. The more he rode the red horse, the better he got. Some of the winnings paid for the next rodeo, some for evening at Curley's, and the rest went into savings. David didn't have the grades to go to a big college, but he could get into a junior college in Denver, maybe Arapahoe Community College. Graduation day was coming and David was looking forward to what was to be his best rodeo season ever.

In April, David and his dad went to the auction, they needed another horse for his dad and were selling some calves. As they were looking at horses, they came across some that seemed better than the rest. A young Mexican man was putting a saddle on a horse, then taking it off and moving on to the next, just to show these horses were already ready to go to work. His dad picked out several in that group to bid on and then struck up a conversation with the young man. His name was Juaquin Torres. He was from Baja of Mexico and worked with his grandfather rounding up wild horses and breaking them. They came to this auction together and Juaquin introduced his grandfather. He didn't speak English but both David and his father heartily shook his hand. His family was very poor and the horses fed his family all year. David asked Juaquin how he learned to handle the horses the way he did. He pointed at his grandfather and said he was a Supai Indian and they have a special way with the horses and taught him how to train them when he was a young boy.

David liked the young man. He spoke with perfect English but shared an interesting view of the world. It seemed as though nothing got him down. The rest of the auction went well, all of the calves were sold and at a nice price. David's dad got one of the horses and they went to load her up to take home. She was a beauty, white with red freckles. She was tall, had sturdy legs, and a surprisingly short mane. With just a whisper from Juaquin, she walked right into the trailer. David's dad then mentioned to Juaquin that David was going off to college and would he be interested in a job at the Ironwood Ranch. Juaquin spoke with his grandfather and then returned to them to say yes. He got his things from the old pickup and hugged his grandfather, then he hopped in the Chevy with David and his dad and rode back to the ranch. His mom was sure surprised; she expected a new horse, but not a ranch hand. She shook his hand and told him he could take meals with the family and could stay in the little bunkhouse. She reached into a closet and got out sheets, blankets, and pillows and handed them to David, told him to get Juaquin settled, and then bring him back in an hour to wash up for dinner.

The bunkhouse was a small log cabin close to the barn. It had a bathroom and six bunks for the seasonal workers and a wood-burning stove. Juaquin settled in and made his bed. He pulled a chair over to his bedside and took a picture in a homemade picture frame out of his bag and placed it on the chair. It was a picture of his mother and he never left home without it.

Juaquin washed up and combed his hair at the bunkhouse then joined David and his dad for the walk back to the house for dinner. That night, it was pork chops and a big bowl heaped with mashed potatoes, gravy, and peas. Juaquin took only one pork chop and that's when David's mom got up and heaped a lot of food onto his plate. She told him that he needed his strength to work at the Ironwood Ranch. They ate in silence but as she cut the apple pie into big slabs, she asked Juaquin about his life. Juaquin's eyes lit up and with a big grin, he told his short story. His English was good because he spent a lot of time in Arizona with his cousins who are Pimas from his mother's side of the family. His family was able to travel to Mexico unhindered by border patrol. They would round up the

33

horses, break them, and bring them to auctions to pay the bills. David asked him if he went to school. Juaquin told him that he did attend the "sister school" but the horses seemed more important as his grandfather got older. He said he would like to go once a year to see his mother and grandfather, but he was grateful for this opportunity. He had such a warm smile and a quick wit. The whole family knew he would be part of their family a long, long time. When the pie was all gone, Juaquin got up and offered to wash the dishes. The surprised look on everyone's faces made him chuckle. David saw the look of delight on his mother's face so he volunteered to help. Besides, he wanted to get to know this young man better. As they started to clear the table and talk, David's mom and dad went out the door holding hands. They were going to go to the barn to visit the new horse, and then walk to the top of the hill to sit on the bench under the cottonwood and watch the sunset over Pikes Peak.

After the dishes were done, Juaquin went to the bunkhouse and brought out a small guitar case he had brought to the ranch with him. He leaned an old wooden chair that David's dad made against the wall on the porch of the bunkhouse and took out a funny small guitar. He put his feet upon the rail and started to play. A sweet sound came out and Juaquin started to sing. In his slow tenor voice, he sang some old Mexican love songs. David sat on the porch of the ranch house and his parents could hear the music at the top of the hill. And Rusty came to the rail to listen to the music.

After graduation, David was busy. He had rodeo and helped at the ranch. He liked spending time with Juaquin. The young man taught him and Rusty some new tricks. Rusty got better and better at calf roping and so did David. Juaquin called him Roja, Spanish for red. He was always amazed that David's hair matched Rusty's and he never missed a chance to tease him. Needless to say, David kept his hat on. One day, they all went into Colorado Springs to buy Juaquin new clothes. He got two pairs of boots, one for working and one for church. He got new jeans, shirts, and a warm winter coat. But what made him really happy was his first authentic cowboy hat. His clothes and straw hat were so worn that he threw them away when he got home except for the hat. He put on his new Stetson hat and cut holes in the old straw hat and put it on Rusty. The horse pranced around the corral while the family laughed. As soon as he could, he rubbed his head against a fence post and off came the hat. Without waiting, he took a big bite out of it. Juaquin rescued the hat while saying something in Spanish to the horse. No one knew what he said but every time he did, Rusty would turn his back to him and that made the family laugh some more. The straw hat was hung on a wall in the tack room in the barn and was there still.

Juaquin went to a few rodeos with David's family, but he mostly spent time at the ranch. He competed in a few things but left the rodeo thing to David. Sometimes he would go to Curley's with David and his friends. Curley and Chet would make him drink his beer at the bar so the boys wouldn't be tempted to have some. Chet would come out from behind the bar and tell stories about his navy days and he always ended up telling the boys to never join the navy; it makes you drink. Everyone laughed when he said it, and after a while, the boys would finish the sentence for him, "It makes you drink." Juaquin was a little afraid of Curley but he liked Donna. Sometimes, he would talk like her on the way home. He said she had the voice of a mountain lion.

Summer was coming to an end and two of David's friends were getting ready to go to college. One in Greeley Colorado and one in Arizona on a football scholarship. David's mom had sent his paperwork to Arapahoe College in Littleton and was getting ready to take him to Denver to find some housing. Juaquin was there to help at the ranch and it was important that David felt good about leaving to go to college. But before any of that could happen, they got a letter that would change all of their lives. David got drafted by the army. There was a war in Viet Nam and he was called upon to serve. His mother was clearly upset and his father told him that he was needed and it was his duty. He joined the army when he was young and remembered going to South Korea. It was the end of that war, but he felt like he had made a difference, he had done his duty. Juaquin walked around giving him a funny salute and told him not to worry, he would take care of Rusty and keep him trained.

That weekend, the boys went to Curley's one last time. David's other friend announced he got his draft notice, but it was too late, he had joined the marines. He said he didn't join the navy because it makes you drink. They all had a good laugh and on the way home, David told Juaquin that he will miss his friends, Curley's, Chet, and even old Curley himself. The rest of the ride was quiet because what David wanted to say was, he also would miss Juaquin, his parents, Ironwood Ranch, and Rusty. He didn't say it out loud, but he felt the loss in his heart. It would be one of many.

Chapter 4

Summer was over and David was scheduled to go to basic training late September. All of his friends had either gone to college or in the service. He was scheduled for six weeks of basic training at Fort Benning, Georgia, took a little break to go home and back for Infantry School. Then to Fort Ord, California, for deployment to Viet Nam. There were a couple of other guys from his senior class leaving at the same time. He spent the time helping his father and Juaquin fix things around the ranch and he wanted to help his mother all he could. He was getting to be very good friends with Juaquin. Sometimes he would go with Juaquin for long rides after dinner just to spend time with Rusty, and sometimes they would ride slowly while Juaquin played his guitar and sang the Spanish songs his mother had loved so much. They would ride to the top of the hill where the cottonwood sheltered a hand-carved bench his father had made for his mother. The view to the west was Pikes Peak. The sunset behind the mountain and it would make the prairie grass shine a soft golden color. The bench had a big tree carved on the back and his father put a fresh coat of varnish on it every year. In the summer, his mom would put an old quilt and pillows on the bench and have a picnic with his dad. They called it prairie date night and David knew he needed to stay away from them and let them enjoy their evening.

The time had come to go, David's parents drove him to Denver to report and the whole trip was spent in silence. They left early in the morning and even stopped for breakfast in Castle Rock on the way. They arrived around nine and he was scheduled to leave at ten thirty. His parents got out of the truck and at one time or other, one of them was holding to their only son. His mom wrapped her arms around him, or his father had his arm resting on the young man's now broad shoulders, or was tousling his hair. When someone came to take him to the staging area, both his parents hugged him and silently got into the truck. They were almost to Colorado Springs where they pulled over at the scenic overlook of the Air Force Academy to watch the planes take off and land. They stood at the front of the truck and just held each other. They both cried a little that day as if their hearts were breaking; their son became a man that day and he would never know just how proud and sad it made his parents. David's dad had joined the army and knew what basic training would do for his son. He would come home for a short visit around Thanksgiving between basic training and infantry school. His dad knew he would not be the redheaded, fun-loving boy that was hanging out at Curley's with his friends. He knew he would be a taller young man. He was going to miss the boy.

The time flew by and David arrived on a bus in Colorado Springs. Juaquin was there to meet him. He barely recognized David. The red hair was getting darker, darker than Rusty's. He shook his hand so hard that David thought he would break his arm clear off. Then he did the funny salute, then he talked the whole way home. David only had four days and tomorrow was Thanksgiving. Juaquin talked about all the food they were making as if David hadn't eaten the whole time he was gone. Tonight was fried chicken and his mouth watered as Juaquin described the food. He had taken over helping David's mom in the kitchen and was learning how to cook and even showed him a few new things. Juaquin stopped the old Ford outside the gate and David got out to open it. He got a tear in his eye as he looked up at the hand-carved tree branch over the gate and committed it to memory. It was a beautiful way to welcome him home to Ironwood Ranch. He opened the gate and let the truck drive through and then slowly closed it again. As he turned to get back into the truck, he saw it drive away. He thought Juaquin was playing another joke on him, then he saw something in the distance. It was Rusty, all saddled up and running to meet him. It was as if he knew he was at the gate. The big red horse stopped and nuzzled David. He couldn't stop hugging and petting his horse, and it took a good ten minutes to climb up and start the walk towards home. He couldn't imagine a better welcome than this, but he got home and saw the banner and balloons all over the house. His parents were on the porch waiting for him and he barely made it onto the porch before they were hugging him. Rusty got a few carrots and went to get a drink while the family went inside. Juaquin was helping David's mother set out the chicken and fried potatoes and his dad told him to wash up. David couldn't stop smiling. He loved ranch talk and missed the family a lot. He mostly missed Rusty; the horse was his best friend. Dinner was full of stories about the town, the neighbors, and what was happening on the ranch. They laughed, ate, and were happy. No one even thought about him leaving in a few days. It was a holiday and he was home; that's all that mattered. David was very tired but wanted to take care of Rusty. He went outside with Juaquin and when the ranch hand whistled, the horse came over to them. It made David laugh. They took him to the barn, removed the saddle, and brushed him down. All without saying a word. David slept like a rock that night. He had the best chicken dinner in the world and got to sleep in his own bed. He did notice that it seemed smaller but you never forget comfort. He had a nice Thanksgiving and spent some time with Rusty. His mother drove him to the bus station when he had to go. She hugged and kissed her son, and she told him to come home in one piece and to write. Then she handed him a couple of spiral notebooks that would fit in his shirt pocket and a handful of pencils. David asked her what he was supposed to do with the notebooks. She told him he would know. And if he needed more, he would let her know. He handed him something else. His dad's staghorn pocketknife. She said it makes the best pencil sharpener, but someday, it might save his life. By then, the bus arrived so she kissed her son one more time and held his face with both her hands as if to memorize every inch of it.

It was hot and humid in Saigon Viet Nam when David arrived on a C-130. It made him unusually tired but after a few days, he got used to it. He spent a couple of days at Tan Son Nhut Airbase then was attached to the 199 Infantry at Long Binh.

He started out writing letters home every day but eventually, he ran out of things to say so it was once a week, some things he couldn't and wouldn't write about. He tried to find something funny to write about. One day, he was out with his platoon and it came to him why his mother gave him the notebooks. They stopped to rest and David took out the first notebook and broke a pencil in half. He put one-half in his pocket and sharpened the other half with his dad's pocketknife. Then he dated the first page and started to write. He wrote about the people, sights, smells, and most of all, he wrote about how scared he was. He wrote small and used both sides of each page so as not to waste any space. These notes were for him to see only. He would continue to write to his family, but his real feelings were safe in the notebook. He didn't write in the books every day and one notebook would last him two months. When some of books were full, he would send them to his mother and ask her to just put them in his closet. She would send more. His mother never read his notes.

The first year passed quickly. Things changed there and there was talk about the troops going home. David continued writing his notes. There were friendships formed in that thirteen-month stint with other ranchers and rodeo fans. Word got around fast and you could tell where they were hanging out because they played country music. But there were also losses. David wrote about the losses in his notebooks. He saw horrific things in that war. Things that no human being should see. He found that he wasn't frightened if he wrote it down. He always wrote a note to his mom on the first page and his address in Calhan. Sometimes days would go by without writing and sometimes he had to write several times in a day. When his thirteen-month tour was over and he had a chance to stay, he found out that he didn't need to. They were slowly pulling troops out anyway. He went back to finish his time at Fort Ord and go home. He was excited to make the long-distance phone calls and hear his family's voices. That was the only time that David felt so homesick that he cried each time he hung up.

The rest of the time flew by and he finally got to go home. He took a bus home and was wearing his uniform the entire ride. When he got on the bus, someone on the bus spit at him and called him baby killer and other vile names. He stayed at the back of the bus where he thought no one would see him. It

41

only made him grow quieter and quieter. He sat next to another soldier. He asked him where he was going and was told home to Arizona. David felt sorry for the other soldier, a Hispanic boy with big, brown, troubled eyes who looked out the window into the dark and cried softly. He saw from the ribbons on his uniform that he did more than one tour in Viet Nam but he decided to not talk about that place. In the daylight, they talked about cars, girls, and movies until they arrived in Winslow. The young man got off the bus and into the loving arms of his family. David had wished him luck. The rest of the trip was spent in silence. For some reason, the young soldier made him a little sad.

By the time he got to Colorado Springs, he was tired from no sleep and was determined to not speak of his time in the army ever again. He was proud to serve like his father and now the whole country wanted to shame him. This time, it was his dad that picked him up. He was standing there when he got off the bus and grabbed his duffle bag. He patted his son's tired face and, without a word, took him to the truck. There was a plaid snap shirt and his cowboy hat in the cab and David was never so glad to change his clothes in his whole life. After he put on his shirt and hat, he was able to finally relax. They stopped for a big burger before leaving town and David had two milkshakes; strawberry and chocolate. He was finally able to muster up a big smile for his dad and promptly fell asleep in the truck before even leaving Colorado Springs. His dad drove slowly and missed all the bumps he could so as not to wake his son. He had read the news and watched TV and was sad that his son went through what he did. But deep down, he knew the ranch would be good for him.

The first few weeks that David was home, he rode every day. He rode the fences as far as he could. He rode the arroyos and the canyons. He would even ride to the cattle, sit, and watch the calves. He just wanted the silence and peace. Sometimes he was angry, sometimes he was sad, and sometimes he just didn't know how he felt. Loud noises bothered him now and so did the quiet. He would listen to the wind and sometimes cry. He would tire of the quiet and go listen to the herd. But the chaos of their conversations bothered him too. He started to take his notebooks and an unsharpened pencil. He kind of chuckled at his mom for buying so many but now he knew why. He still wrote in the small print but he had a lot of thoughts to work through. There were times that he would be gone overnight and his mother would worry, but his dad told her to let him go. If he was hungry, he would come home, but he had to be alone with his thoughts. He would come home with a full notebook on those trips. He would stuff them in his sock drawer at first, but his dad had a better idea. He took him out to his workshop and took all of his woodworking tools out of the large wooden box they came in. After lightly sanding the inside to get any oils out, he gave the large box to his son. The box was about 24 inches square and 8 inches deep. It had a little lock on it and was perfect for his notes.

After a while, Juaquin would tag along David and in silence, they would repair a fence or just ride. Sometimes, Juaquin would take the guitar and play a little but mostly, they were quiet. They would come back hungry and take care of the horses and eat a big meal. The kitchen wasn't the same, it was too quiet. So, David's mom would turn on the radio. She also noticed that her son's hair turned a dark shade of brown, more like hers, and that made her sad. He looked so grown up now.

Eventually, David's friends heard he was home and started to come around. He had been at home a couple of months before he agreed to go into town for a cruise and a burger at

Curley's. He was old enough to have a beer now, but his dad cautioned him to only have one. Chet was the only one there when David walked in and he gave him a hearty one-armed hug. When asked where Curley was, his face got serious. Curley had a stroke last year. He was finally home with his wife, but it was touch and go. He probably would never work again. All of the boys were sad and when the Pepsi came, they all raised their glass in a toast. Chet kept them all busy for a few months, but the boys began to drift off. Some went to college and some moved to Colorado Springs to get a job. Some never came back from Viet Nam and it weighed heavy on everyone's mind. David decided to go to Denver. He would take some classes at the community college in Littleton like his mother planned and try to lose himself in the city. He packed up his old Ford and drove to Denver to find a place. He found one, a furnished basement apartment a few blocks from the college. It was okay, but David stayed to himself so much that the weekends were too lonely. He would go to the ranch on Friday after class and ride Rusty. He would eat good food and go to church with his mom and every evening, he would sit on the porch, watch his parents go up the hill to sit on their bench and listen to Juaquin play and sing. He would cry sometimes but mostly he found some peace in his heart. It felt good to him. The second semester was a little more difficult and in one of his classes, he met a girl. She helped him with his math and invited him out to parties at night. One night, she invited him to go all the way to Larimer Square in downtown Denver. They went to a little bar in a basement and listened to jazz music. David had a couple of beers but after a while, he found himself unable to breathe. In a deep panic, he ran outside. The air there seemed heavy too and he couldn't get enough air into his lungs. He got into his truck and drove to

Parker where he pulled his truck over and got out to take a deep breath. He sat on the tailgate for a long time, looking at the stars and breathing. That was the hardest thing he ever did. It wouldn't the only time David felt that way. Eventually, he gave up and left the city. He was looking for a place he could be happy. After living in Colorado Springs and even in Pueblo, David returned to Calhan. He found a place in town to live and got a job at the co-op feedstore. During the week, he loaded feed into the backs of pickups for the ranchers and on weekends, he hit the rodeo circuit. He had a couple of friends that went with him, and he would go get Rusty and the old trailer and go. They went to Wyoming and all over Colorado and even New Mexico. He even went to Cheyenne Frontier days where he met a bronc rider named Chris LeDoux. He was a songwriter and would sell tapes of his music. Rodeo music and the life of a cowboy. David liked the music and bought several tapes. He would roll down his window and play Copenhagen so loud that he swore Rusty could hear it in the trailer. The boys won some and lost some and all in all, the money kept him able to rodeo. But at each one, David would stand with the rest of the cowboys at the arena resting his boot on the bottom bar and would watch the bull riders. He memorized their every move and tried to mentally imagine the bull's next move. Some were predictable and some were just wild. He wanted to ride but could hear his mother's voice making him promise he wouldn't. Before the rodeo at the Adams county fairgrounds outside Henderson Colorado, David and his friends were hanging out at Curley's. They talked to Chet and each other. David told his friends he was thinking of riding. They laughed and teased him. Chet said, "Don't do it." He said that kind of recklessness cost him his arm and if he promised, he needed to keep it.

David got Rusty and the trailer and had dinner with his mom. She kept looking at him as if something was up, but just couldn't put her finger on it. She had a habit of gently smoothing his hat before a rodeo. Her way of giving him good luck. He left after dinner because it was so far to go. It was a warm morning already and David and his friends were signing up for their events. They all noticed a bull named Satan and walked out to take a look at him. They heard about this bull. No one lasted eight seconds on him and most got hurt one way or the other. They went out to his pen and looked at him. He was a brindle bull, red and dark brown. He had one black hoof which made him look even fiercer. He snorted and stomped around the pen and every once in a while, he would throw his weight against the gate. He was big and muscular and kept his head down. David said he looked kind of scary and his buddies teased him again. They said he knew he wanted to ride and called him a schoolgirl. They went back to registration and David decided at the last minute to go ahead. As he nervously signed up for the bull ride, his eyebrow went up. There was an extra two hundred bounty to the cowboy who could stay on for the full eight seconds. RCA rules don't allow the extra incentive, but this was a local event that was run by the State Rodeo Association and wasn't subject to RCA rules. This bull was known all over for not being rideable and people would come just to see cowboys try.

Just before the event, the draws were posted and they all went to see what bull David drew. He was at the bottom of the list.

Satan. It was too late to change his mind. He could stop right there and pay the turn out fee, but he didn't.

He went to his events but listened to the cowboys around him. There were a lot of side bets going on by the pens and that made him more nervous. He borrowed a pair of chaps from one of his friends and went to get ready for the ride. He thought of his mom, but would use the extra money to buy her something nice. By the time he reached the pen, Satan was so worked up he was kicking and no one could get close to him.

David got onto the bull and grabbed the rope with his gloved hand. The rope was a 9-plait Barstow bull rope with an old smashed cowbell on the bottom. The glove was rosined up and ready to go. Satan was so big around that once the rope went on, it had a real short tail on the bull rope. There wasn't much for David to wrap around his fist to get a good hold. He did the best he could but was even more nervous.

The horn sounded and the gate opened. There was no hesitation on Satan's part. All four feet were off the ground as he shot out of the gate. Everyone scrambled out of the arena. David lost all sense of motion and sound. It was as if the world stopped. The only thing he could hear was the sound of his own heartbeat. The next thing he knew, he was on the ground and felt a sharp pain in his chest and left leg. He could still see the bull coming at him and tried to roll out of the way and that was the last thing he remembered. He woke up in the ambulance as they were shutting the doors, and his friend handed him his hat and promised to take Rusty home. And just as the door closed, he heard him say he did it. Eight seconds. Then he didn't remember anything else. It all seemed like a slow-motion dream to him. He woke up in the hospital three days later. Four broken ribs, a broken ankle, and a concussion. He could see his mother talking to the doctor. He had never seen that look of anger on her face before. She was asking if he would ever walk again. The doctor couldn't say. He pinned the bones back together but had never seen an injury like that. His mom stayed with him for the ten days he was in the hospital. She didn't speak to him about the ride. He didn't bring it up because he had never seen that look. He tried to apologize once and she told him that it was okay, but for the rest of his life, he should always remember the promises he made and to keep them. Life is full of broken promises and eventually a person couldn't get past it. It could break a person's spirit. He just nodded and cried and held her hand. She knew he was sorry. When he was well enough to have a cast and learn to use crutches, he got to go home. He went to the ranch with his parents and Juaquin. He couldn't ride Rusty but Juaquin did and then let the red horse come to the porch to get carrots from David's hand. One Saturday, David's friends came to the ranch in the big old Chevy sedan and asked him to go to the rodeo. The car was comfortable and they would help him around. His father told him to go and said it would be good for him. As they drove away, David could see his mother in the mirror. She waved at him and he waved out the window back at her.

The El Paso County fairgrounds in Calhan were packed that day. It would be the last one at that arena. David and his friends sat on the lower bleachers closest to the arena. Just before the bull riding competition, the gate opened and out came a familiar bull, Satan. He was a brindle bull, a combination of Angus and Brahma. His red and dark brown brindle hide culminated into a fierce, dark, enormous head that looked almost black, making his horns look ivory. He stood bigger than most bulls and seemed even taller at his huge muscular shoulders growing into a solid hump. He scared the children and most adults.

He slowly walked around and David struggled to stand. He managed to get to the fence on his crutches and stood there looking at the bull that caused him so much grief. Satan lowered his head and ran out of the arena. The announcer came on, introduced Satan, and then introduced the young man who rode him. David waved one of his crutches in the air as the crowd cheered. After the rodeo, there was a dance, but David was still on the mend and wanted to go home. Juaquin came to get him and sang a song he learned on a Chris LeDoux album for him, "All Around Cowboy." It made David smile and go to sleep. His rodeo days were behind him for a while. He couldn't wait to get well enough to go back to his apartment and back to work. But on that time, the rest and Rusty time was what he needed.

The next day, a package showed up addressed to his mother. In it was a ceramic statue of a bull and a hammer. She could do whatever she wanted with them. After she laughed with him, she picked up the hammer, placed it on the mantle, then placed the bull right next to it. It would stay there for a very long time.

David got well fast; he soon was out of the cast and using a cane. With help, he got on Rusty but couldn't rest his foot in the stirrup. He pulled it up so it wouldn't hit his old friend and the big gentle horse took him for easy, slow rides. There was a big surprise on the ranch. Rusty sired a foal; he was a nice brown velvety color Sorrel with a white star on his forehead similar to Rusty's marks. He was wrinkly and wobbly the day he was born. David wanted to call him Dan, but his dad said Old Dan and it stuck. Old Dan was a funny little guy and had a funny habit of herding the dogs and even Rusty around the pens. David fell in love with this little guy and was with him as much as he could be. Rusty was getting a little older and this horse was going to be a good ranching horse. He would come out on weekends to break Old Dan and eventually ride him out with his dad to tend to the cattle. Rusty didn't seem to mind

David riding on Old Dan. Some days, he liked to just stay in the pens and beg David's mom for carrots.

Finally, David moved back to his apartment. He pretty much stuck to himself and worked and went to the ranch. He was still on his cane when his friends started to talk him into going to dances. Sometimes he went and sometimes he just stayed home. The silence was comforting and David still had attacks where he shook and had trouble catching his breath. No one knew and being alone helped. He would turn off the lights, open the curtains in the kitchen, and sit and look out at the stars with the window open, gulping in the fresh air. He would free his troubled mind and think about a late-night ride on Rusty.

The attacks would go away, but they were always followed by bad dreams and sleepless nights.

Chapter 5

It was almost a year before David could go back to the rodeo again. Rusty and Old Dan helped to rehabilitate him, but the fracture was slow to heal. He started to practice team roping with his friends and found that Rusty had a real knack for it. Old Dan wasn't ready to ride so he was allowed in the pens just to practice. He was fun to watch and had more of a knack for it than Rusty. The boys would do team roping close to town. If they had to go out of town, David would make his excuses and stay home. He would then practice calf roping at home, hoping to make a comeback, but his injuries slowed him down a bit. Rodeo wasn't the same for him. But he liked being there. He liked the people, the announcer, the judges, his parents, his friends, the horses, the livestock, even the cheeseburger at the snack shack. So, when he was needed, he would help out as a pickup man and even run the chute gate as long as it wasn't a big bull like Satan in there. Staying home at the fairgrounds was more to his liking these days. He spent a lot of time at the ranch and started to write in his notebooks again. Healing was a two-part process, his bones and his head. Writing helped. He had healed enough to start going to the dances. He loved the old country music and cowboy songs and loved to two-step. Some of the girls there could dance and some were shy. He even asked a few to the dances. He liked it when his parents went. They were good dancers. He suspected they practiced a lot when he was a boy. He used to hear the big kitchen table slide across the floor and good country music would play softly. He never got up to look. He respected their privacy, but he was sure proud when they took to the floor. They were both getting close to sixty that time and looked great.

One day in August, David went to the rodeo and then to a dance afterwards. There were a lot of folks there that evening. People he hadn't seen before. He and his buddies were having a beer by the door when he saw his mom coming his way. She looked very pretty that night with her hair down. She had a twinkle in her eye and was holding the hand of the most beautiful blonde girl he ever saw. She had her hair in a ponytail with a few strands streaming around her face. She had on a pretty pink dress and flat red shoes. In fact, she was the only one in the grange hall that didn't have on cowboy boots. She had a curvy figure and the nicest blue eyes. He kissed his mom's cheek and then she introduced them. Her name was Ruth. Such an old-fashioned name. His mom said she was the new teacher at the school, teaching ninth and tenth grade. She had taught in Denver but if she was here, her student loans would get paid. Ruth said she always wanted to live in a small town and everyone chuckled. They were bored in this town but she seemed to be so excited. The music started and David asked Ruth to dance. She shyly admitted to him that she didn't know how to two-step but was willing to learn. After explaining the steps and demonstrating to her with his mom, Ruth and David went out on the dance floor. She caught on fast and he would tell her what it meant when he would press on her waist or shoulder and she was able to keep up. They spent the evening dancing and laughing. When the last song played, he walked her to her car and said good night. But as he opened her car door for her, he asked her if she would like to go out next week. There was a dance at the American Legion hall in Ramah, the next town to the east. She said yes and thanked him for making her feel welcome in town. David felt great as he walked the few blocks to his small apartment. When he got there, he didn't turn on the lights. He just sat in the window and thought about the teacher he had just met. For the first time since he got home from Viet Nam three years ago, he didn't feel like he couldn't breathe, and for the first time in a year, his bull riding injuries didn't hurt. He was almost thirty then and that night, he felt at peace with the world. He opened his drapes over his bed, looked at the stars like he did when he was a boy on the ranch, and fell asleep with a smile on his face.

All of David's friends gave him a hard time on Thursday night when they were having cheeseburgers at Curley's. Chet gave him some advice that made all the boys laugh but seriously wished him well. Chet knew the hard times the young men went through in the war and many times he offered a caring ear to listen to their issues. Most of the boys got married and started families, but David was different. He didn't want to talk about what he saw and what he experienced in Viet Nam. He wanted to push them away and cope the best he could. He went into the service a nice boy with red hair and sparkling eyes and came out a brown-haired man with shadows in his eyes and a smile that hid how he felt. He jumped at loud noises and couldn't hear as well as he could before. Chet worried about this one. But now, there was a girl. Chet caught a twinkle in his eyes now and then.

Dave and Ruth spent the weekend driving around town and to the ranch. He showed her the market and took her to Curley's for a burger. They went to the auction, to the fairgrounds, and even to the train station. She liked the streets named Boulder, Denver, and Golden. They walked some of them and looked at the cute houses. She stopped at a little white house on Boulder Street. It had a big front porch and was small and Victorian. The picket fence was cute and she told David that that house was her favorite. They went to the Paint Mines Canyon and took a walk. He asked Ruth if she liked the badlands-type chalk canyon, and when she nodded, he said there was an even more colorful one on his parent's ranch. On Sunday, David and his mother picked Ruth up and took her to church with them. She looked very pretty with her red skirt and white blouse. Her ponytail had a green ribbon and looked very golden in the light of the stained-glass window. After church, she rode to the ranch with them for chicken dinner. Juaquin sang some songs on the porch while Ruth helped with the dishes. He promised her to take her for a ride the next time she came if she would bring some jeans.

David started to write in his notebooks about this new someone in his life. He would go to the ranch and ride Rusty and write. The tone of his writing took a wonderful turn. He started to carry the notebooks and shorthand sharpened pencils in his shirt pockets all of the time. He didn't want to miss a thing.

The next few months, David and Ruth spent weekends together. They must have walked around the small town several times. It was only a mile long so there wasn't much to see. One weekend, they drove to Limon and had lunch at the truck stop. Several times, they drove to Colorado Springs. They went to the zoo and walked all over Manitou Springs. They even drove to the top of Pikes Peak. David tried to convince Ruth he could see the tree that his parents sit under to watch the sunsets. At first, she thought she could see it but soon realized he was joking. David made Ruth laugh. A strange giggle that was unique to her. He could pick her out of a crowd by that giggle. He also made her blush. He would kiss her and she would turn red and smile for hours and sometimes, a sweet sigh escaped from her lips. When he was with Ruth, all the bad memories from his past left his head. And at night, he would lay in bed, look out at the stars, and softly hum to himself. He no longer shook till he cried at night. He never felt a need to talk to her about it, he just knew he felt good finally.

Ruth liked David. During the week, she would think of him often and look forward to the weekends. The kids never got homework on Fridays because she just wanted to think of him. When he touched her, she would smile for hours and his kisses made her insides tingle. She didn't think about love, but she was having the time of her life. Ruth had boyfriends in college and afterwards, but none kissed her like the kiss would protect her from the world. David grew a mustache while he was recovering from the bull ride injuries and he was so careful when he kissed her, so protective. His kisses were so tender that she never felt the mustache. She did think it was odd that his mustache was red and his hair was dark brown, but when his mom showed her his rodeo pictures, she saw his red hair and understood. It only made him more handsome to her.

The very best part about spending time with David was her Sundays at church and then to the ranch. The gate had a huge tree carved up one side and the branches stretched across to the other side. The Ironwood Ranch was becoming her second home. She took her jeans and would learn to ride. Sometimes, Juaquin would go with them and they would ride the fences or go to work the cattle with David's dad. And sometimes David and Ruth would ride in the canyon that ran through the property. It was more colorful than the Paint Mines, but the colors would change at different times of the day. They would be extra careful since David had the run in with the rattlesnake but sometimes, they would just sit in the prairie grass above the canyon and watch the sun on the formations. If they were on the ranch on Saturdays, they would ride down to the gate to get the mail. Out there, the mail was delivered by housewives. They would have the old family station wagon with a magnetic sign on the door that said "US Mail." Most of them did this while their children were in school and some did it only in the summer and drove school busses the rest of the year. The woman who delivered at Ironwood Ranch was David's friend's mom. She still had kids in school, and David liked to go see her when he could. His friend didn't make it back from Viet Nam and David liked to touch base with her. He was very proud to introduce the pretty, blonde girlfriend to her. Ruth loved the ranch. She was learning to cook from both David's mom and Juaquin and was having fun in the enormous kitchen. Winter was coming and she was a little upset. She thought that would mean no trips to the ranch. But snow never stopped a rancher and they made it every weekend. Ruth learned how to make a Thanksgiving dinner and she learned how to prepare leftovers. Her idea was to burn them a little and feed them to the dogs. Juaquin would laugh at her antics. December arrived and Christmas was coming. Ruth had only known David for a few months and as she spent the cold nights in her little apartment, knitting a warm scarf for him, she came to realize she was falling in love with him. His kisses made her feel warm and safe and when she would touch his face and run her finger along the brim of his hat, she would hold her fist closed as if to capture and hold the memory there forever. She wanted to be with him forever. This small town captured her imagination and David captured her heart.

David felt the same way about Ruth. He was planning a big Christmas surprise for her. Everyone at the ranch was in on it and this year was unusually festive. His dad went to the mountains by Elbert to cut some trees for decorations. One was the Christmas tree in the living room and one he chopped branches off, wired them into garlands, and draped them on the porch rail, the fireplace, and even the bench on top of the hill. The house smelled of freshly cut cedars and the tree was a majestic blue spruce. He even stung a few lights outside for Ruth.

Ruth didn't know if she wanted to ride in the winter. She was riding Rusty by then so David could ride on Old Dan. Dan stood taller than Rusty and was a rich velvety brown and was soft to the touch. The first big snow came at Halloween and the ranch was very pretty the next day. The sun was out and the snow sparkled. The pine trees looked festive and it was very cold. Ruth dressed warm and got on Rusty after Juaquin saddled him. To her surprise, the horse was very warm. She relaxed and rode with David to look at a spot on the fence that had so many tumbleweeds tangled in it that some wire broke. After it was fixed, they rode back to the house, the horses kicking up plumes of fine snow behind them. David stopped several times to just look at her and to bend way down to kiss her. His hazel eyes reflected the snow and Ruth could almost see herself reflected in them. She told him that winter riding was her favorite. She was hooked on the way it made her feel so alive and never missed a chance to go for a ride on Rusty.

Christmas Eve came and they decided to stay at the ranch for the night. David's mom and dad decorated the guest room for Ruth with evergreen boughs, shiny ornaments, candles, and piled lots of warm quilts on her featherbed. But the big surprise was yet to come. They opened gifts that night. Ruth got pots, pans, and wooden spoons. David gave her a pair of warm gloves to ride with. She gave David her handknitted scarf. She had stitched a tree that matched the tree carved on the gate on it. David put it on and wore it all night. Ruth noticed a gift under the tree wrapped in red foil with a silver ribbon that had her name written on the tag. David said that was a special gift and she had to wait till the next day. Christmas morning, they had a wonderful breakfast and went out to go for a short ride. Three horses were saddled because David's dad said he had to check on some cattle. David had his scarf on and made sure Ruth had her warm gloves on. Off they went to take a picture of the canyon in the snow. They didn't want to be gone long because Juaquin and his mom were preparing a huge feast. On the way back, they rode to the tree on the hill. The day was clear and Pikes Peak was beautiful with the snowy peak against the clear blue sky. David stopped and helped Ruth off of Rusty and took her to the hand-carved bench. There were several festive quilts on the bench and a thermos of hot chocolate with cups and a small plate of cookies. Right in the middle was the red present addressed to Ruth. That was where David's dad was going that morning. He even decorated the bench with evergreen. It made Ruth happy and she took pictures of the festive scene. They sat on a quilt on the bench and covered their laps with the other one. David took the cups and thermos out of the basket and poured them both a steamy cup of rich, creamy hot chocolate. They got out the plate of homemade shortbread cookies in the shape of trees and dipped them in their cups. The view was wonderful. When their cups were empty and packed away, David stood up and reached for the shiny red box. It was about six inches square and for a minute, Ruth thought it was the coffee mug she admired at the western wear store. Then David took the quilt off of her lap and put it on the soft snow in front of her. He got down on his knees and, with a choked-up voice, told her that he couldn't imagine living life without her and that one time, his mother told him that a broken promise makes a broken heart. So, if she would be his wife, he would promise to love her till he died. Then he gave her the box. Ruth shook as she opened the box. Inside was a small ring box and David took it out for her. He opened the box and there was a beautiful diamond and sapphire ring. Ruth started to cry when he took the ring out, took off her glove, placed it on her finger, and asked her to marry him. The word yes squeaked out, but became louder and louder. She kissed and hugged the man who loved her and cried on his shoulder. They packed up the blankets and basket, got back on the handsome horses, and rode home where they were greeted with eggnog, hugs, and kisses. This was may be the best Christmas at Ironwood Ranch.

The rest of the winter was a blur to both of them. Preparations for a wedding next summer were underway. They would have it at the ranch with a huge barbeque and a dance in the barn. David, Juaquin, and some of David's friends started to fix up the barn. His dad made benches for the ceremony and dinner to take in the barn for the dance. They all went to Denver to visit Ruth's mother who was in a wheelchair. There were arbors to build, flowers to plant, and a dress to buy. David would buy western slacks, a white snap shirt, and a string tie. He also bought a new black Stetson with a silver leaf and turquoise band to match his tie. His dad hired temporary ranch hands to help with the cattle and fences because, for some reason, there were a record number of calves born. At one time, there were seventeen hands staying in the bunkhouse and David's mom had to hire another person to cook. The wedding was the weekend after the Fourth of July rodeo. Luckily, school was out and Ruth was freed up to finish up the planning. The ranching community, friends, teachers, and everyone in town was talking about the event. It was going to be an event unlike any other in Calhan.

The day came and the sky was clear. It was cool out and that was perfect. Juaquin and some of the ranch hands built a big fire for the barbeque and all of the rest of the food was ready. Instead of a cake, there were pies. Peach was Ruth's favorite and apple was David's, but there were so many. It was like going to the county fair; everyone brought pies. Ruth drove to the ranch with her dress carefully laid out in the backseat. The gate had been decorated with flowers and ribbons that gently blew in the cool breeze. She was glad it wasn't hot that day, she was so nervous that she was hot. The gate was open and she was greeted with a sign that said "Ruth and David." The drive to the ranch had little stands of flowers and the whole porch was decorated with the vining hibiscus in purple and white that David's mom grew. There were benches, flowers, and a huge arbor with a table and bible in the middle. Ruth started to cry when she saw Rusty wearing a wreath around his neck, but broke out in laughter when she saw he tried to eat it. She was careful to not see David before the wedding and parked her car at the back of the house. She placed her gown in the guest room and went into the kitchen. The wedding was in a few hours, she had to dress and put on her makeup. She would wear her hair in its usual ponytail but would wear flowers and ribbons on it. In the kitchen, she saw David's parents. They were sitting at the big table that was full of sweet-smelling pies and seemed to be saying a prayer. They both grabbed her hands and asked for blessings on this happy couple and then they hugged her so hard she couldn't breathe.

They wanted to welcome her into the family by themselves before the ceremony.

After her preparations, she stood at the door waiting for David. All of the guests had arrived and were seated. The pastor was under the arbor and both of David's parents were standing there with him. There were no bridesmaids nor groomsmen. This was a simple ranch wedding and only the bridal couple stood in front of God and tied their lives together forever. David was at the bunkhouse. He arrived a half hour ago. Rusty was tied up at the bunkhouse and had managed to not eat the flowers on his neck. All eyes were on the bunkhouse including hers. The door opened and out came a very handsome cowboy with his hat in his hand. He stopped and looked towards the farmhouse then put his hat on and climbed onto Rusty's saddle. He slowly rode to the arbor then got off and walked to the pastor. He was kissed by his parents and when they were seated, he turned to look at the house. Juaquin had learned the bridal march and played it on his guitar. Out came Ruth and she slowly walked to the arbor. Her dress was tea length and simple. She had flowers in her hair and a bouquet of pink roses and baby's breath in her hand. Then David looked down and saw the sweetest thing, Ruth had a pair of white cowboy boots. She wanted to show David and his parents how much this way of life meant to her.

After the ceremony, the barbeque started and a mariachi band started to play. They were some friends of Juaquin and were in town for the Fourth of July rodeo. It was their gift to the happy couple. The mood got very festive as they started to play for the guests. There would be a western band playing for the barn dance after dinner and it would be a day that everyone talked about for years.

Ruth was renting a room from another teacher in town. She had no furniture at all so she moved in with David after a honeymoon in Santa Fe, New Mexico. She shopped a little for decorations and art for the house. They had been looking for a house to buy for a few months. David took her into the post office to change her address and introduced her to Barry, the postmaster. He had an earring in one ear and was single. He shared a very nice, large Victorian house with his mother till she passed away and he turned the garage into a workshop. Ruth liked him right away. He knew so much about the town and was so fun to talk to. She found out he was an inventor. He once converted his mother's car so it ran on steam. He also collected comic books and the kids liked him because he knew everything about them. Mostly, he made Ruth laugh and showed her the comics he got.

Barry also knew everyone in town and the houses that were going to get sold. Ruth found one on Boulder Street and would pass it every day on her way to school. Of all the houses in town, she loved that one the best. It was all white and had a large porch with rockers on it. There was a tiny yard with rosebushes and yellow flowers. On the corner was a bay window and she imagined her desk in that window. From the outside, she could see it had a fireplace. She wanted to knock on the door and ask to see the inside but was too shy. Every time she was at the post office, she would ask Barry what houses were for sale. He gave her all the dish about what was wrong with each of them, but told her nothing was wrong with her dream house. Then one day, about three months after the wedding, she went to the post office for her mail and the dish about the houses. Barry first told her there was a very big one by the train tracks but it was too noisy, then he winked at her and said the white house on Boulder Street was going to be listed in a few weeks. She really should go knock on their door and make them an offer. Then he wrote the asking price on a piece of paper and handed it to her. Ruth hugged Barry and kissed his cheek. She invited him to dinner and then ran all the way home to tell David.

Three weeks later, the house was theirs. They made a trip to a furniture store to buy what they needed and a couple of weekends at garage sales in the city. They had gotten so much stuff at their wedding that it was all stored at the bunkhouse and Juaquin was happy to load it all up and take it to them. He had a special surprise for them too. He had learned to paint from David's mom and painted a beautiful picture of Rusty and Old Dan running through the tall prairie grass with the sun setting on Pikes Peak behind them. It was a large picture and took the place of honor in the living room. After they were all moved in, Ruth wanted to cook a nice dinner for her husband's parents. They had done so much for her and even taught her how to cook. It was Saturday and they arrived at her house with Juaquin. The newlyweds ran out to the driveway to welcome them all into their home. Something was in the back of the truck and was covered with a tarp. David tried to peek but was told he could see it after dinner. Dinner was wonderful. Ruth even made a large blueberry pie for dessert. After the last dish was washed and put away, they all went out to see what was in the back of the truck. David's dad pulled away the tarp and what they saw made both of them cry and hug his dad. There were two rocking chairs for the bare front porch. His dad had hand carved the Ironwood tree on the back of each one and the legs and crossbars looked like branches. He had varnished them so they would hold up to the weather and they were a shiny honey-colored wood. On her seat was their initials carved in a heart. On his seat was the Ironwood Ranch brand burned on it.

They were lifted up and placed on the porch. Ruth sat in her chair and felt like it was made to cradle her body. She closed her eyes and imagined all of life's events this chair would get her through.

Chapter 6

Years went by, the couple was happy in their house. No children came to them, but they had each other. David still worked at the co-op and weekends at the rodeos. He still wrote in his notebooks and put the pages in the wooden box. Ruth liked the short walk to school. They bought a new truck a few years ago and decided that they really don't need another car. The weekends that there was no rodeo were either spent at the ranch or in the city stocking up on supplies for both them and the ranch. David's parents didn't wander too far away from home. There were more cattle and they had hired a few extra hands.

Curley passed away and the whole town turned out for his funeral. The reception was at the bar and Chet had many stories about his best friend. David and his friends were all in their forties then and all had many stories of Curley and Chet. None of them drank, thanks to the bartender, and they all took a minute to remember their friends who never made it home from the war. Even though he was celebrating his best friend's life, Chet had a sad look and a couple of days later, there was a sign on the door of the bar. It was closed for good. Chet moved back to his hometown. He said his farewell in the note. He loved Calhan, but it would never be the same without Curley. They served breakfast and lunch everyday over at the auction, so David had to get his cheeseburgers there. Winter came that year and the weather was bad almost every day. Some days, David took the truck out to drive his wife to school even though it was just a block and a half. The prairie grasses looked scrubbed clean from the blowing snow and it was constantly piled up on the fences. The ranch hands were working day and night to keep the cattle in hay and keeping ice out of the stock tanks. David sometimes went out on sunny days to check the fences but didn't worry too much since the cattle tended to stay close to the house. Rusty was too old to ride then and only wanted to stay in the barn with the dog for company. Old Dan was taller and more muscular and seemed to do better in the snow. There were other horses on the ranch but Juaquin and David preferred this big horse. Late one night, several years ago, there was a phone call. Rusty was down. He was pretty old and had a long life, but David's mom wanted him to come say farewell to his friend before he passed away. The couple drove in the storm to the ranch and both cried the whole way. Not a word was spoken. When he got there, Rusty could barely lift his head but made an effort when he heard David's voice. Ruth hugged his neck and whispered her good byes and left her husband to sit in the straw and hold the beautiful horse's head in his lap. Tears were streaming down his face, but everyone left him to be alone with his best friend until he passed. In the morning, coffee and breakfast were on the table when David came in. Rusty had hung on till dawn and went with a heavy sigh. The whole family and Juaquin sat at the table to say a prayer for the horse that brought such light to the family. Each one of them had loved and been loved by that horse. He was David's big brother and helped him recover from the war. They were all grateful.

The winter was still cold and snowy. The sunny days were so bright that it hurt your eyes. January was clear and dry but still cold. Perfect weather to go to the National Western Stock Show and Rodeo in Denver. David's parents had not been there in a long time, so they decided to stay at the Brown Palace Hotel for a couple of nights and make a vacation out of it. They had a great time until the third day. It started to snow, a little at first, but the wind blew too. After the auction that afternoon, they decided to start the drive home. Hopefully, the storm will stop at the Palmer Divide like it usually does and it would be smooth sailing the rest of the way home. The drive was so slow, ten miles an hour in some spots. It took two hours to just leave Denver.

David and Ruth went to the ranch for the weekend. But his parents were on the way back, so they decided to go back to their house. They had to go to work the next day and it was nice to sleep in their own bed.

It was around 2 am when they both heard pounding on their front door. Ruth got to the door first and looked out. She saw Barry, the postmaster, on the porch. She opened the door and saw what a blizzard it was outside and pulled him inside. He only walked a few feet from his car to the porch and was covered with snow. She grabbed a blanket off the couch, dusted him off, and took him to the kitchen where David met them. When Barry was dried off and warmed up, he told them he had his police band radio on. He couldn't sleep and decided to listen in. There was a terrible accident on Monument Pass and several people were killed. He heard that someone from Calhan was in the accident. He knew David's parents were on the road that day and he asked them if they had called them to say they got home okay. Ruth said nobody called and went to the phone to check if it worked. They heard the dial tone and as she was putting the phone back in the cradle, they heard a loud knocking on the front door. David went to the door and noticed flashing lights outside. There was the local state trooper and the El Paso County sheriff deputy that also lived in town. They both came in and David invited them into the kitchen. Before they could start talking, Ruth and Barry started to cry. David's parents were driving home and came upon an accident. They both got out of their car to offer some assistance and were struck by an out of control semi. They both died at the scene.

David sat down and started to shake. Both officers knew his family well and gave their condolences and asked if there was anything they could do. Ruth asked them to stay a while with them and made coffee. No one rested that night. Barry made breakfast for all of them and kept the cups full. Ruth sat as close to her husband as she could and fought to not fall apart. Her husband needed her and she loved this family so much. David just sat and shook. Sometimes he would talk about his parents and even talked about breaking the promise to his mom about the bull ride. He had a hard time believing any of it. The trooper offered to take him to Colorado Springs the next day and set it up for noon. They wanted to try to get to the ranch to tell Juaquin in the morning.

The next morning, the snowplow came down their street to help them get out to the street. The sheriff's car and trooper's car fell in behind David's truck and they followed the snowplow all the way to the ranch and even to the house. Everyone left and David and Ruth talked to Juaquin. He was heartbroken but told the ranch hands and rode to town with the kids. When they came into town, the whole town turned out on the streets to wave flags and show their respect.

There was a beautiful funeral. The town was full of cars, most had to park at the fairgrounds and a school bus took them to the church. It was packed and a large tent was outside with heaters and speakers to accommodate all the people. There was a caisson with horses to take the caskets to the cemetery and everyone walked behind it. It was a pretty day and most of the snow had melted. The sun made it feel warm and the graveside services were short. The ladies at the church made a nice meal and reception. After it was all over, David shook Juaquin's hand and sent him back to the ranch. He and Ruth walked home and sat for a while facing the western sun in the hand-carved rocking chairs. He had not cried through this whole time and Ruth was concerned. Her eyes were swollen and red from the loss of her in-laws. David started to talk about the day his dad bought Rusty. He got halfway through his story and couldn't keep it in anymore. He went inside with Ruth. She held him and comforted him, but his sobbing came from a deep place. He would cry for days and wandered around feeling lost. Then Ruth gave him his boots and hat. A trip to the ranch was needed. They didn't go to the house. They just got on the horses and went for a ride. The fresh cold air brought him around and soon the lines on his face were gone. Old Dan was just the medicine he needed. After the ride, they brushed the horses, fed them, got into the pickup, and went to town. Juaquin understood; they couldn't go to the house yet.

For the next few months, the ranch was run by Juaquin and the ranch hands. He would go to town for food and supplies and check in at the feedstore with David. Finally, a lawyer in Colorado Springs called David. He wanted them to come to his office with Juaquin to read the will. Time had passed, but it was now time to talk about the ranch. The three of them met with the lawyer and he read the will. His parents left him almost everything. Juaquin got two horses and the old truck. They also wanted him to stay at the ranch for the rest of his life if he wanted to. The loyal ranch hand took a rather large bandana out to dry his eyes. David's dad left the big kitchen table and the bench at the top of the hill to his beloved daughter-in-law. His mother left her some jewelry, pots, and pans. She also left her the handmade quilt she slept with her first time at the ranch. All of it meant so much to Ruth.

David got the money his dad managed to save and the ranch. He wasn't sure he wanted it. The lawyer put his arm on David's shoulder and said he knew it's hard, but he should go to the ranch, get familiar with it, and make the decision. He was ready to put the ranch up for sale, but didn't want David to make a decision he would regret later. David promised Juaquin he would be there all next week. He had some thinking to do. Juaquin understood but felt compelled to tell David that the ranch missed him too.

Saturday was shopping day, so he and Ruth stocked up the truck and made the drive to the ranch. It was a very pretty drive south of Calhan. There were other ranches, all neighbors of theirs. The road was hilly and it seemed they saw a different view with every hilltop. It takes about an hour to get there on good days, down the highway, and a left turn on a dirt road. Today was sunny and it seemed that the drive was very short. Soon, they saw the cattle in the south pasture. Then they got to the hand-carved gate and David stopped to get out and open it. He looked up at the massive carving of a tree that his father had done. Below the branches was the word "Ironwood," and on the trunk was the brand. He had kept it varnished and it was a soft honey color. David had never really studied it before and noticed the details, the leaves, and knots in the branches. Ruth drove the truck through the gate while he stayed behind to close it back. Just as he latched the gate, he could see Old Dan slowly walking down the road. Juaquin had trained him to go get the mail when he heard a vehicle. David's mom sewed a pocket in his horse blanket and would put a carrot in the pocket. When he got the mail, the mail delivery person would take out the carrot, feed it to Old Dan, and replace it with the mail. When the horse saw it was David at the gate, his ears perked up and he started to run. David was so happy to see his buddy. His soft, brown, velvety coat felt unusually good under his hand and for the first time, he noticed the horse's brown eyes had flecks of gold in them and seemed to sparkle in the sunlight. He got in the truck and reached through the window to grab the reins. They slowly went up the drive and when they got to the porch of the house, David pat Old Dan while Ruth went inside to find a replacement carrot. The horse still had to go get the mail. When he left, David slowly carried the groceries into the house. Juaquin had been in there and opened the curtains and put on a pot of coffee for the two of them. David thought it would be hard to look around, but he started to feel comforted. It was as if his parents were just up on the hill and would be back any minute. Ruth started to get things ready to make dinner. Tonight, it would be his mother's recipe for fried chicken. She missed them so much. She was cooking while David made a fire and walked around the house. The smell of apple pies and fried chicken floated around the house and he found his mouth starting to water. He built the fire and took a long look at the carved mantle above the fireplace. It was similar to the gate. A big tree with leaves. Today, he noticed something he had not seen before. Hidden in the leaves was a tiny squirrel. He went into his room and got out the wooden box with the notes. He had left it there because he wrote fewer notes and would just deposit them during his visits. On the sideboard was a large pack of new notebooks and a note on top of them in his mother's handwriting that simply said "David." He took out a notebook and found a hand-sharpened pencil in the box and sat in his dad's big chair and started to write in his tiny print on both sides. By the time Ruth said it was dinnertime, he had filled two books with memories of his mom and dad, and he seemed to feel a little better. His mother was right; he would know when he needed the notebooks. Juaquin took the homemade fried chicken to the ranch hands and came back to share dinner with his best friend. The mashed potatoes and gravy were steaming and the chicken was crisp. There was pie and coffee. It tasted just like they all remembered but to David, it was his mom's slice of heaven. He couldn't remember tasting anything so good. He loved his wife for doing that. David didn't feel like talking at first but when Juaquin started to tell Ruth stories of the parents, her husband chimed in. Soon, they were all laughing and sharing funny memories. After dinner, they sat in front of the cozy fire while Juaquin played a few songs for them. He had learned some new things and it surprised David when he played some Chris LeDoux songs. He ended his day feeling better, and some of the deep sadness had lifted. His taste buds came alive over dinner. He was looking forward to what the next day held in store for him. He and Ruth had a big decision, but when he gazed at her sleepy eyes and the half smile on her lips, he knew what her decision would be. He only hoped this wouldn't let her down.

The next day, David and Ruth had coffee on the porch like he had watched his parents do. The sun was coming up on the plains and the tall grass seemed to be waves of orange in the morning breeze. The ranch came alive in stages. The chickens and dogs were first. Juaquin fed them all and they were awake and active. It was warm that morning. As the sun got over the horizon, the horses were moving about and getting ready for the morning work. Old Dan was saddled already and turned loose to go to the house. He got a withered carrot from the root cellar for his effort this morning. David made a mental note of bringing a large bag from the feedstore for his faithful horse. Ruth was wanting to ride that day but knew her husband wanted time alone. She went inside to take the fresh biscuits out of the oven and make a large amount of sausage and egg sandwiches. She wrapped several up along with cold chicken for David and filled his canteen with cold freshwater. He would be gone all day and would need the energy. Juaquin got a big pan of sandwiches for the ranch hands and they rode off to tend the cattle. There were so many calves this year and they needed to all have a check up and get a brand. Work went on at the ranch. He wished David luck and asked him to stop and see what they were doing while he was on his ride today. David went inside for a new notebook and pencil then he and Old Dan left. The two of them would be making decisions today and there would be a lot of writing in his notebook. Ruth joked that she needed to put notebooks on her list of supplies. She kissed her husband and left in the truck to go get supplies. As she walked to the truck, David watched her. They had been married for years now, but he never got tired of seeing her in Ropers and jeans. Her signature blonde ponytail blew in the breeze and he took out his notebook. The first thing he wrote was how much he loved her and how he hoped she would have that ponytail forever. She turned to wave at him and he swore her blue eyes sparkled to reflect the sunlight. That day, he noticed things at the ranch he never noticed before. Her eyes were one. The large front door with the tree carved in it was the other. He never noticed how majestic yet welcoming it was.

Old Dan smelled of hay and carrots and his soft velvety skin made David think of the velvet drapes in the living room. They took off towards the fences and would cut back to the north pasture where all of the calves were. The smell of the damp grass and the sun on his face made David smile for the first time since his parents died. He stopped at the bench under the big tree and made a note in his book. The first day's ride was as if he was seeing the ranch for the first time. The sights and smells. He rode along the fence and then turned towards the pasture. The grass wasn't tall yet but smelled sweet and was very green. He arrived at the pasture and spent time roping and branding calves. Separating them from their mothers was a trick, but Old Dan was up for it. He forgot the horse knew his stuff. Soon, he was yelling and waving his hat and laughing at the calves with the other hands. He had forgotten how nice that was. They wound it up and as they headed in for lunch, he decided to ride some more. There was so much to see on the ranch. He rode by the east fence where there were some old buildings and some new haybarns. His dad was going to take the buildings apart to use the old barnwood in his woodworking shop. David had not gone into that little building yet. He stopped and made a note to get it done and while he was doing that, he made a note of how the hay from last year still smelled sweet and how the warm sun and slight breeze felt on his face. He ate his lunch while sitting on a bale of hay and watched Old Dan snack on it too. What a beautiful horse he had. He was a cocoa-brown sorrel and was taller than Rusty had been. His back was broader and David had to buy him a better fitting saddle. He went to the feedstore in Kiowa and found it on sale. It belonged to a young Morgan and was big enough for Old Dan's broad back. His hair was very shiny in the afternoon sun and was soft as velvet to the touch. The white star on his forehead was more of a cream color. David's dad said it looked like a marshmallow in a cup of hot chocolate. His hooves were also bigger than Rusty's were. His step was always sure.

David liked to brush this one. His defined muscles rippled under his velvet skin.

When he was done, he rode towards the canyon. The canyon was like an arroyo that ran across the northwest side. The cattle didn't go that far but he liked to go there. He rode in at one end and it dead-ended about four miles to the west. At first, it just looked like a simple arroyo but when it opened up, there were chalk towers. Some were yellow and some were red. Some were brown with white tops. Some formed caves and narrow walkways. All of the colors were the colors of a sunset in the desert and today, the colors were so bright that they hurt his eyes. Even he was on Old Dan, he was careful to leave before the sun started to set so his horse wouldn't lose his footing and stumble. There was also more dangerous wildlife in the canyon such as diamondbacks and mountain lions. He was remembering the early days when he took Ruth for a ride there. She loved the chalk canyon and said it reminded her of fairy castles. It was more of a maze and a person could get lost in there. David's dad always kept the cattle away from the entrance. The colors were so many. Some were yellow and some were orange and white; they reminded David of his favorite ice cream treat. And some were brown. Last year, David and Ruth went on a picnic in the canyon and found a hidden gem, a blue formation.

After he left the pretty canyon that was starting to change colors in the afternoon light, David made a beeline towards the house. The ranch hands were cooking out on the grill tonight and he could smell the smoke all the way to the canyon. At one point, the cool air in his face made him want to run Old Dan. The big horse seemed to sense it and when his rider leaned forward in the saddle, the horse took off like a bolt of lightning. His silky mane blew in the wind and his long legs made him look majestic while he ran. He slowed down as he got to the barn. Juaquin took the horse inside to clean him up, feed him, turn him out, and told David to go wash up. Before he could leave the barn, David walked around and took a long look. The horse stalls were clean with fresh hay and the door at the corral end was wide open. There was a wooden floor down the center aisle that had been hosed off and smelled damp and clean. He took the saddle from Juaquin and put it away in the tack room. His mother had organized that room and everything always had to be put back where it belonged. The large clean window looked out towards the house and David could see Ruth on the porch waiting for him. She was beautiful with her golden ponytail. He had never noticed the house before. It was large and a single story. It started out as a large kitchen with a wooden stove, one bedroom, and a bathroom. David's dad had built onto the house and now it had four bedrooms, two bathrooms, and a large living room with the biggest hand-carved mantle on the fireplace. The outside was a nice honey-colored wood with a porch that went around three sides. That way, they could always be either in the sun or in the shade. It had posts and rails around it so the horses could be tied there if needed.

The front door was the centerpiece of the house. It was very big and had a giant tree carved in it. There were two oval windows and some of the leaves overlapped the glass. The kitchen had a Dutch door that his mother insisted on. She could have fresh air and the dogs would stay outside. The sun was going down as he walked towards the house. Even as he stepped onto the porch, he knew what he was going to ask of his wife.

After dinner, they both went out to look at the stars and listen to Juaquin play the guitar. His funny old guitar broke a couple of years ago and David sent away for another one. The sound was deeper and warmer than the old one. Juaquin played all the time now. As they sipped on coffee on the porch, David remarked how pretty their rocking chairs would look on it. His mom and Ruth spent three weekends braiding rags into a rug for the porch and he recognized some of his childhood whippersnappers woven into the rug. Ruth nodded and said she could spend every mild evening out here in her pretty rocker. He got up, kissed his wife, and went to get the coffeepot. When he came back, he was startled when she asked him if they could keep the ranch. She had practiced almost the same speech as he did all day and he decided to let her have her say first. She said she could drive to school and it would only be an extra hour. And while she was in town, she could buy groceries and maybe even feed and supplies. When she finally took a second to catch her breath, she saw David was chuckling. He confessed he wanted to ask her the same thing. Ruth was so excited; she jumped in his arms and almost knocked the pot out of his hands. She let him go and said this was home to her.

That night, David wrote more in his book. All he had to say about how he felt about the ranch took up a whole book and at the very end, he wrote that he loved his wife in tiny letters that barely fit. He put it in the box and went to bed. There was much planning to do and he couldn't wait to tell Juaquin.

The next day was full of excitement and planning. Ruth had a big notebook with plans. The attorney was invited to lunch and Juaquin made three peach pies. No one was happier than he was that day.

There was the house in town to rent out and moving to do. But before all that could be done, David had to go through his parents' things and pack them away. There wasn't much, but he wanted to put them in the hand-carved cedar trunks his dad made. Ruth was so excited to move and call the ranch home. She moved so much when she was a child that there was no place like this. She was humming while she was cooking and making her to-do list. She had to go back to work on Monday and it was already Thursday. She had some artwork to hang on the bare walls here and was planning where everything would go. Her love of this ranch was almost as much as the love she had for her husband. The first thing she did was go out to the porch and decide where her chair would go.

The little white house on Boulder Street was rented out and everything was moved. David quit his job and worked at Ironwood Ranch full time. He was very happy there. Old Dan was his constant companion. Juaquin was training new horses and there were new calves. Ruth helped out and cooked for them and Juaquin and the three full-time ranch hands. This was a big year for calves. His dad had added more cattle through the years and was smart to add more hands. Moving them from one pasture to another was a big undertaking that time and sometimes they needed more hands. Juaquin helped to maintain the buildings, horses and other animals, and gardens. He helped to cook and was putting the finishing touches on what would turn out to be the biggest barbeque grill in the county. Since Ruth was going to continue to teach, the extra cooking help was appreciated. Ruth returned to school. She would get up early, fix breakfast, and drive the hour or more into town to teach. In the evening, she would stop at the post office and the store and co-op if needed before heading home. David decided to get her a bigger car to do all of these chores in. Sometimes his wife would come home late and that was when Juaquin would jump in and cook for him and the crew. There was a spring storm that put three feet of snow on the ground throughout the day and Ruth didn't make it home until one in the morning. But summer came and she was happy to not leave the ranch except for getting supplies in Colorado Springs. Every morning after breakfast and coffee on the big porch, she would put her new Ropers on with her Levi's. Her long blonde hair would go up into a ponytail and then off she would go to the barn to help out or to garden, or sometimes she would take Juaquin's mild-tempered black mare out to the pastures to help David and the crew. She would pack food and drinks and meet them in her new pickup, or she would just spend the day cooking and canning the way David's mother taught her to do. Her skin would take on a warm glow and the sun would make only one or two freckles on her tender nose. These were the days she loved the most. Long sunny ones with her husband by her side. But fall would come and for a few weeks, she would cry on her drive to the school. It was so hard to leave the ranch.

Several years went by, the ranch was making money and David was very happy. Last winter, there was a surprise in the barn, a new foal. She was Old Dan's and looked like his father, Rusty. She was a pretty red color with white feet and a white mark on her forehead that looked like a long-stemmed white rose. Ruth named her Rosie. She would follow Ruth around like a puppy and made her laugh. Juaquin was breaking horses that summer and he was wanting her to be with him. She was a very funny horse, since she seemed to understand Spanish. Juaquin would get excited around the horses and would speak

79

Spanish. Rosie seemed to understand him. The whole ranch liked this horse. She was a free spirit who thought she was human. Sometimes she would push open the kitchen door and walk right in. She didn't have time for the dogs, though. It made her nervous to have them underfoot. When the dogs came near, she would freeze and if she had a foot up, it would stay there till she knew the dog was far away from her. Like Rusty and Old Dan, she was allowed to go anywhere she wanted. She stayed close to Ruth, though. Ruth had carrots, apples, and other goodies. One time, Rosie went into the kitchen and ate all of the fresh peanut butter cookies Ruth had made for the church bake sale. She was angry with the horse and yelled at her. Rosie hung her head and left for the barn. She didn't leave the barn for three days until Ruth came and got her. She took her to the porch, gave her two apples, and sat and had coffee with her. Ruth felt bad for making this precious young horse hide from her and wanted to be her friend again, so they talked all afternoon and had coffee and apples and finally, the beautiful red horse let Ruth rub her and hug her neck. They found their trust again and Ruth never yelled at Rosie again. She was still standing by the porch when David came back from the south pasture. He shook his head but smiled and was happy his girls made peace.

That summer was a tough time for Ruth, she didn't want to go back to work. She didn't want to leave the peace and serenity of the ranch, and she had suddenly become so very tired. Anytime she had to drive to the springs or Kiowa, she would come home exhausted. It made her unusually sad to leave and happy to be home.

David and Juaquin had a lot of horses the last two years and it was time to break and sell them. Horse Day at the auction was coming up and Juaquin wanted to make a lot of money to get a new truck. They only kept enough horses to work the ranch. It seemed David was at the auction in Calhan or in Greeley. He was selling an unusually large amount of cattle this year.

Chapter 7

Ruth quit going to the auctions with David. They hired big trucks to come get the cattle and horses. David always went to the giftshop or over to the fairgrounds to find a craft or small gift to take to Ruth. Several times, he would come home and she would be sound asleep on the porch with dinner simmering away in the oven. She barely made it through dinner sometimes. David built in a dishwasher for her but sometimes, he and Juaquin would clean up. She would beg to stay home on weekends and seemed to be extra quiet and tired. Summer was coming to a close and it seemed the closer it was to school starting, the lesser she spoke. Her face still lit up when he walked in the door, but she never let him talk about her going back to work. Juaquin saw how tired she was and asked to drive her to work and back a couple of days a week. He would go into the springs for supplies and then get her at three on his way back. He was always buying extra fruits or juice for her and it seemed that Rosie always got the leftover fruit. The drive into town and back was unusually quiet and sometimes she just fell asleep in his truck. He tried to chat with her, but she would just stare straight ahead and didn't seem to hear him. David noticed the changes in her. Her eyes were blank and she wouldn't talk anymore. Most of the time, she stayed up late grading papers and he would find her asleep on the couch in the morning. He wanted to hold his wife again, brush her long hair, and go for rides and walks. Mostly, he missed sitting on the bench at the top of the hill and watching the sunset on Pikes Peak. One day, David was walking through the kitchen and noticed Ruth's gently worn Ropers on a towel by the door. Mud was still crusted on them and he knew they had been in the same spot for weeks. She loved her cowboy boots and took such good care of them. He picked them up and took them out to the porch to scrape the mud off, clean them up, and even polish them for her. As he worked on her boots, he noticed how worn they had gotten, even a spot by the heel in the back. That was where she rested her feet on the porch railing when she sat on her rocker to have coffee. He noticed she didn't do that much anymore. By the time he was done, the leather was soft and supple and ready for their owner's tender feet. He put them back but made a note to keep an eye out to see if she would put them back on.

It seemed like Ruth would get home later and later from town. And when it snowed, she would arrive home around eleven. David was always asleep so another night went by with his wife sleeping on the couch. As the school year went by, it became worse. Sometimes she would sit at the table and just have a blank stare. David didn't know how to talk about this. He just hoped she would snap out of it. He missed his wife. After a while, he just gave up. She clearly didn't love him anymore and he wasn't comfortable talking about it. He did try a few times but became shaky and had to go outside to gulp in the fresh air under the stars. Winter came and went and it was soon early summer. The ranch smelled of grass and wild flowers. David picked a bouquet of pretty, fiery red Indian paintbrushes, yellow sunflowers, and even a few purple columbines for Ruth. He put them in a mason jar on the table for her. She didn't say anything, just gave them a blank stare as if she didn't know what they were. Then she got up from the table, scraped the food off the plates into the garbage disposal, picked up the jar, and emptied it in there too. She finished cleaning up and went to the living room to rest on the couch. The cattle operation was really starting to pick up. They were keeping more calves and even hired more ranch hands. Juaquin called some of his nephews to bring their horses and work there too. The bunkhouse was full and it gave Juaquin time to do the gardening that Ruth had stopped doing. He was very puzzled. Sometimes he would mention to David that she was pale and not strong, but David didn't know what to say. He would just shrug his shoulders. The only things that Ruth seemed to enjoy on the ranch were cooking and Rosie. There were several times he would return to the house to find Ruth reading to Rosie in the kitchen. He would shoo her out and ask Ruth what she was thinking. She would just go outside and take Rosie back to the barn.

School started again and Ruth was gone and was even more tired. David asked her to go see her doctor, but only a couple of times. Finally, he gave up. One Saturday, she was sitting on the porch with coffee and the paper reading to Rosie, who would take the pages out of her hands and noisily chew them up. David wondered why he hadn't seen a paper in a while. If he tried to take the paper away from the horse, she would stop and lick his face like a puppy. He gave up. After the game with Rosie, he asked Ruth if she could listen to him for a few minutes. She looked at him and focused on what he had to say. She looked so pretty with the afternoon autumn sun in her blonde hair. Her skin was pale and she had put on several pounds that he had not noticed before. He took a deep breath and told her that there was no need for her to come all the way home from work anymore. The little house in town was empty and he thought she should move. He told her to pack what she wanted to take with her and he and the ranch hands would take it to the house. At first, he thought she was going to say something. He saw a glimmer of sadness in her eyes. But she just got up and went inside. She didn't speak a word. For the next few weeks, David would hear her crying, but she would not let him see her.

Before the snows came, she was moved into the little white house on Boulder Street where they started. Her rocker was back on the porch. She decided to walk the few blocks to the school and David would see her almost every weekday when he would go to town. He knew at around three, she would be out walking. She started to lose the weight and she would wave at him when her hands weren't full of homework. Sometimes he would stop at her house and drop off mail for her and ask how she was. The ranch was so busy, the sales and rodeos kept him busy on the weekends. David even started going to the dances with his friends. But he never saw her there. A couple of times, he met some girls at the dances; some from Kiowa or the springs. They would go out a few times, but he was really too busy to drive any distance to continue a relationship. He was starting to like time alone on the ranch. He would ride the fences and stay out more than just a day. He wrote in his notebooks about the life he had then. Often, the writing was about Ruth. His best friend seemed to be Old Dan and he would go to town to get large bags of carrots and apples for the horses. More than a year went by, David was starting to feel his age. He got a new truck and Juaquin talked him into buying an old Jeep to drive to the fences. He tried it, but it wasn't the same as a ride on Dan. The cattle took a lot of time. Spring and summer were busy. David would end his day on the porch watching the sunset and listening to Juaquin sing. He would write in his notebooks and laugh at Rosie. Juaquin was breaking her and she would walk around with the saddle on her pack as if she was a model. She would hold her head up high and come see him on the porch for treats. He could tell she missed Ruth, so he kept plenty in the kitchen for her. In the evenings, she would sometimes go stand with Juaquin. He would sing and she would make the strangest sounds and stomp her foot. If David didn't know better, he would have thought she was singing too.

Fall came and the leaves were a bright color this year. The rides were nicer than David had expected. One evening, he arrived back late. It was dark and there were no lights on in the house. Usually, Juaquin left him some dinner and would turn on the lights. After Dan was unsaddled and fed, David decided to look in the bunkhouse. Rosie was outside and seemed upset. He walked inside and saw Juaquin on his bed looking pale and barely breathing. He couldn't get him to answer him when he asked what was wrong. Then he got closer and saw a bite on Juaquin's hand. Rattlesnake. He called for an ambulance and they said they would send a helicopter. After David turned on all the lights at the ranch, he went out to check on Rosie. She was still upset. He could clearly see her hooves now and on the bottom of one of them, he saw something that frightened him. It was the remains of the rattlesnake. The horse must have stomped it to death. He got the hose and washed away what was left. He closely examined the horse and was relieved to see there were no bites. Rosie was taken back to the barn after the helicopter left with Juaquin.

He was taken to the hospital in Colorado Springs where they were able to give him anti-venom and saved his hand. It took a while for Juaquin to recover. Rosie never left his side.

David would go to the auction on Mondays. Sometimes he had cattle to sell, sometimes he would buy a bull, but mostly, he went to keep up with the latest ranching information. After the auction, some of his old rodeo friends would go get a burger and coffee at the café there or at the new one on the west side called Roosters. He would head home about two-thirty and would drive by the school to see Ruth. She would walk the short block and a half home and usually had her hands full. On Tuesdays, he would come to the co-op and on Wednesdays and Fridays, he would make a trip to town to the post office. It seemed like a perfect place to catch up with the town news. On Thursdays, he would go to Colorado Springs for supplies and would time his return to drive by the school. Lately, Ruth would be walking slower and sometimes, he would park and help her with her heavy bag of papers to grade. They walked in silence and he would leave as soon as he put her bag on the porch. Her hair had gotten a little dull and seemed thinner. Sometimes she had it down. She always had a ponytail so at first, David didn't recognize her. Her eyes got a little dark around them and she seemed way too thin. Some days, he missed seeing her but felt she must have had to stay to help a struggling student.

Juaquin got better and was the one who went to town a few days a week, so it came as a surprise to David seeing Ruth one afternoon struggling to walk home. Her hands were empty yet it seemed that great effort was taken to put one foot in front of the other. He sat in his truck on the corner and watched her slowly make her way up the street to her house. She didn't seem to notice him watching her. When she got to the gate, she stopped and rested her hands on top of the gate then rested her head on her hand. David was about to get out of his truck, but she pushed the gate open and went to the porch. Ruth rested at each step then let herself into the house and shut the door.

The next day, she seemed a bit more normal so he just assumed she was just tired.

It was spring and the calves needed to have vaccinations and brands. That was a very busy time at the ranch, so David and Juaquin only went to town for supplies and hurried right back. Spring was warm and beautiful that year. The trees blossomed and the Russian olives that grew by the fence smelled extra sweet. The grass in all the pastures was a bright green and was getting long fast. Some afternoons, there was a short rain shower and those were the best days for David. He would go up the hill after the rain and just breathe the smell of the rich, wet earth. Sometimes on Saturdays, David and Juaquin would ride to the canyons and enjoy the bright colors of the little cutaways and caves. David loved the canyon; he would come there as a boy to draw and when he started to keep notes, he found solace in the hidden gems. He brought Ruth there and fell in love. The memory was so strong that he wrote about it every time he went there. He sometimes swore he could see her shiny blonde ponytail swing behind her as she ran behind a rock to hide from him. He didn't think he still loved her or that he missed her. He thought about how she didn't love him and he sometimes would pray that she would be okay.

That weekend, he got to go to the canyon both days. Old Dan wasn't a fan of the curves and hidden caves. But he loved time with David. When David would dismount, he would stay close to him. On the second day, they brought Rosie along. She seemed to be very nosey and enjoyed a game of hide and seek. She would hide behind a rock and wait for David to come find her. She would hide her head and think he couldn't see her even though the rest of her body stuck out the other side. Old Dan would go up behind her and give her a nudge, but she waited for David. On the way home, David got Old Dan up to a nice trot. The wind felt good on his face and right next to him was Rosie. Of course, she had no rider, but she moved very fast. Sometimes she would get ahead of them and stop to kick her front feet in the air as if to say to hurry up. Then she would get very still and wait. When they were abreast of her, she would take off again. Her antics made David laugh.

The next day was auction day. David looked forward to Mondays. He would get a breakfast sandwich at the snack bar and a big cup of coffee. He always tried to get there early so he could enjoy the quiet before the crowd came. From the snack bar, he could see the school. Sometimes he could see Ruth walking towards the doors but not that day. The auction was over around noon and after lunch and iced tea with his friends at Rooster, David headed back towards the ranch. As usual, he drove by the school. He parked on Boulder Street so she could see him and wave but she didn't show up. He waited a little longer and drove home. That night, he called her but there was no answer.

The next day was co-op day. He needed to get some pellets and treats for the horses. Also, he needed some rope for Old Dan's bridle. He stopped again on his way home and Ruth wasn't there. By Friday, he became concerned and decided to ask Barry at the post office if he had seen her. Barry and Ruth were good friends ever since he helped her to decorate the house on Boulder Street. He would know about her. Maybe she was on vacation. When he walked in, he could tell something was wrong. Before he could ask, Barry started talking. Several times he had to tell him to slow down. Barry said that Ruth had missed school for a few days, but yesterday, she went. It took her almost an hour to walk the block and a half and she was late. Someone had to open the door for her and when she walked inside, she collapsed. The fire department sent paramedics, but they were afraid to move her. A helicopter came to the fairgrounds and very carefully, everyone who could helped to carry her to the waiting helicopter and gingerly loaded her on it. They were afraid to jostle her or do anything that might make her stop breathing again. David's eyes were wide open and he had to make Barry repeat the story before he understood. He told David that they took her to Penrose Hospital in Colorado Springs and he should go as fast as he can. He was crying as he begged David to go. He handed him the phone to call the ranch and let Juaquin know and asked him to call him when he knew something. Ruth was Barry's best friend and he was so worried. David had the new truck and was able to get there in less than forty-five minutes. He checked in at the main desk and found out Ruth was in ICU. He didn't like hospitals and the alcohol smell made him nauseous, but he hardly noticed it that day. He almost ran to the ICU and when he arrived, he spoke with the nurses before they let him in to see her.

The nurses told him that Ruth had become run down for years. She had a few things that made her ill but never recovered. David was shocked. He lived with her and never knew she was sick. Then they said that her job and working in the summer took its toll. She became so sick, run down, and weak that she developed pneumonia. She tried to rest but thought she was needed at work. That was when she collapsed. He asked how she was at that moment. The nurse shook her head and said they couldn't even tell him she would make it through the night. David entered the room. Ruth was on a respirator and looked so small, frail, and weak. He sat down and held her hand. It was cold and so small. He started to talk to her. He told her to get well. To fight and get strong and he would be there to help her. She was not alone. After a while, she opened her eyes and managed to squeeze his hand back. He stayed all night with her, only leaving her side to get a drink or call the ranch. He even gingerly laid down on the bed next to her then held and comforted her. He tried to get all of his strength to go and help her make it through the night. He still loved her and didn't know it until he held her in his arms and prayed for her.

About midnight, the doctor came in and listened to her lungs. He told David she was improving and to keep praying. David prayed through the night and fell asleep holding her in his strong arms. Two days later, she was breathing on her own and had a tighter grip on his hand. Juaquin came to the hospital with clothes for David and sat with Ruth while he showered and changed. Ruth was feeling well enough to sit up a while and her face lit up for Juaquin. He brought his guitar and played a little song he wrote about a silly horse who eats peanut butter cookies. This made her smile.

As she got stronger, she decided to talk to David. She told him how tired she was and it got worse for her. How she cared for her students, but found that she had nothing left to give at home. She knew she wasn't well, she had to admit to David that she kept it from him. His mother was a very strong woman and nothing got her down. Ruth was embarrassed to admit her frailty. She said the weekends at the house would be spent resting so she could make it to work and she lost that battle. She was sad about losing him. She cried everyday but was so ashamed to admit it. David just held her hand and said it's okay. After a while, they both could smile at each other. They understood.

Ruth continued to get better. David went home to get things ready for her. He told her that he wanted to make her well and asked her to come home with him. She agreed and told him how grateful she was. After ten days, she was allowed to go home with David. Juaquin and David went to get her and take her home. Juaquin got her clothes and personal things from her house. He opened the refrigerator to clean it out and saw there wasn't anything in there. He was so surprised. He would make sure Ruth ate and was determined to feed her till she got all her strength back and was the pretty girl David brought to the ranch. The nurses fussed over Ruth that morning. She was on death's door and then a miracle happened. They brushed her thin golden hair and put it in her signature ponytail. She said she hadn't had one in months and it felt so good. Her dress was too big and the nurses pinned it in the back so she wouldn't look so thin. They met the truck in front of the doors and David carefully lifted her out of the wheelchair and into the truck. Juaquin placed pillows around her to keep her steady and they slowly made their way back to the ranch. The road crews heard she was going home and had graded the dirt road to rid it of washboards and make her ride smooth. The neighbors made food and brought flowers. It was good to have Ruth at Ironwood again.

David called the school and said her recovery was most important and she would probably not be back for the rest of the year. They were so concerned and asked him to give her their best. When he hung up, he felt bad that she would probably never return to teaching. Her health and happiness were more important. He just didn't have the heart to say it out loud to them yet.

Ruth was so happy to be home. For a few weeks, she remained indoors but every chance he got, David would open all the windows and doors to give her fresh air. Juaquin took on the role of cook and soon, Ruth's strength started to return. Rosie heard Ruth's voice and would go to the house everyday as if to stand guard over the woman she loved. After two weeks, David started to carry Ruth out to the porch to sit in her rocker. She was still unsteady on her feet but being in David's strong arms gave her strength. David would spend hours brushing her long blonde hair until it finally started to get that familiar shine. At night, he would rub her thin shoulders and then hold her until she fell asleep. Then he would just lie there, count her breaths, and give thanks that she was alive and with him. While Ruth was on the porch, Rosie would sometimes come up the steps and put her head on the lap of the woman she loved. She was more like a big puppy instead of a horse. But she was so gentle and sometimes Ruth would fall asleep with her hand resting on Rosie's face. When that happened, Juaquin would come out and carefully lead the horse back to the barn. It didn't help, because a few minutes later, she would be back to watch over Ruth.

Ruth got stronger every day and even put a few pounds back on. The doctor would come out to Ironwood to visit her and was amazed at the progress she was making on her journey from death's door. She was able to walk to the porch by herself and to feed carrots to Rosie. Summer was coming, the breeze was warm and the sunsets were spectacular. David would sometimes drive her up to the bench on the hill to watch the sunset over the Rockies. She would be exhausted but happy as she held his hand and rested her head on his broad shoulders.

On the day David heard her singing in the kitchen and saw she finally put her Ropers back on, he went out for a long ride. He took two notebooks that day and filled them up with feelings. All the things that happened the last few years without Ruth, how he told himself it was okay, and how for two years he never wrote a word about her as if she never existed those two years. If he had written about her, he would have seen he still loved her and would have fallen apart. Now he couldn't get enough of writing about her. He sat on Old Dan and wrote on the front and back of each page in tiny perfect letters. He sharpened his pencil with his father's old pocketknife and when there was only an inch left, he took another from his pocket. David would let Old Dan eat some prairie grass and would look all around. When he had almost filled both books, he started to cry. He knew what he had to do. If he didn't say something to her, he would burst. His heart was full and he remembered his mother told him to let it out before it made his heart burst.

It was late in the afternoon when he finally got back to the house. He didn't see Ruth on the porch. He took Old Dan to the barn, removed his saddle, brushed him, and got him fresh food and water. As he turned to leave the barn, he heard a soft familiar giggle coming from the corral behind the barn. He looked in Rosie's stall and saw she was missing. As he stepped out into the corral, he stopped and ducked back into the shadow of the barndoor. He could see Rosie. He also saw Ruth. She was walking the pretty red horse and every once in a while, Rosie would stop and nuzzle Ruth and tickle her neck with a lick. Ruth would giggle like he remembered and reach into her apron pocket to get a big carrot and feed it to Rosie. David didn't want to interrupt them playing, so he backed up and went back to the house. Once there, he put his notebooks away and made two tall glasses of sun tea and went out to sit in the rocker on the porch. Soon, he saw Ruth walking towards him with her golden hair swinging behind her. Her Ropers were dirty and her apron pockets were empty. She was beautiful in

94

her jeans and Ropers and all he could do was smile. Ruth's face lit up when she saw the still handsome cowboy holding out a glass of cold tea for her. She started to sit on her own rocking chair and changed her mind. She sat on David's lap. After taking a long cool drink, she put her glass down and wrapped her arms around his neck. He noticed she put a few pounds back on and no longer felt like a good wind could carry her away. Ruth kissed his cheek and told David how she spent her day and how all of a sudden, she felt better than she had in years.

She wanted to thank him, but when she looked into his beautiful eyes, she could only say how much she loved him. She said if he didn't love her back after all she put him through, she understood, but she couldn't hold it in any longer. David stood her up and stood in front of her. He took her trembling chin on one hand and made her look at him. He told her that she never needed to apologize for saying how she felt. The new rule in the house was to speak up and no one will judge. Then he told her that he never stopped loving her and was so scared he would lose her for good. And if it was okay with her, he wanted to say how he felt now. With that, he got on one knee and said he never could exist another day without her and if she would be his wife again, he would protect her from anything that would come her way again. He wanted to love her until the day he died.

Ruth was so happy, the words just squeaked out. "Yes" came in little whispers and got louder and louder.

Two days later, the minister and Juaquin were on top of the hill witnessing them tell each other just how deep their love went. The only other witness was Rosie. It wasn't the cowboy wedding they had the first time but that time, they both asked

God to help them to remember that moment and to get them through hard times. They knew life would go on...

As they finished their private vows, Ruth reached into her skirt pocket and took out an envelope. She handed it to her husband and he read it then gave it to the minister to deliver. It was a letter to the principal at the school. Ruth resigned.

Chapter 8

The ranch was booming; beef commercials were all over televisions. David had full-time help and the teenagers from surrounding ranches came to work for him during busy times. Summer was always busy, he even hired a cook for the summer. It was the guy named Robert who cooked for events at the fairgrounds and for the rodeo. He cooked basic foods but surprised them with pasta dishes or fried chicken. He was well known for his smoked turkey, so David made him an offer and put him up in his dad's old workshop. He built a kitchen in the one-room house and put in a bed and bathroom. Amazing things came out of that workshop and it showed all over the ranch, from the front gate to the chairs and even the hand-carved hat pegs in the tack room. Now it was put back to use and just in time.

Rosie was being trained by Juaquin and everyone rushed to get through the day so they could watch her antics. She reminded David of Rusty who ate Juaquin's hat. Sometimes the joke would be on her and sometimes it would be on Juaquin. He was getting older now and breaking horses became more of a game of patience. He liked Rosie. He would sing to her to calm her and then speak to her in Spanish. She seemed to know everything he wanted her to do. But sometimes she was the prankster and would take it out on the poor man. He already went through two straw hats because she took a bite out of them. She played hide and seek with him every afternoon and seemed to find a new place to hide every time.

Rosie was a pretty horse and knew it too. She would do anything to get groomed so she could prance around the farmyard to show off for Ruth. Ever since she ate Ruth's cookies, they have been the very best of friends. Ruth was ordering large bags of apples and carrots for her friend. She couldn't ride her yet, but they would spend hours at the porch just happy to be with each other. Most people have pet dogs or cats, but Ruth had a pet horse. On rainy days, the horse would stay in and Ruth would take her coffee out on the porch to see her and even go to the barn. She never missed an opportunity to stroke the horse's silky hair.

As Ruth's strength returned, David decided to go to a few competitions. This time, to compete in cutting. He started to notice that Old Dan was getting very good at cutting calves out of the herd. He really didn't have to prompt him or even guide him. He was a natural. One day, Ruth drove the old Jeep out to where they were all working calves. She spent the morning making peanut butter cookies and ham sandwiches for everyone. They were all way too busy to go in to eat, so she packed up lunch and ice-cold tea and went out to feed all the cowboys. She had started to bake cookies in the morning and made the mistake of leaving the top half of the kitchen Dutch door open. When she walked back in the kitchen, there was Rosie finishing up a plate of cookies. Ruth could never get angry at her best friend, so she took her outside and locked the door so Rosie couldn't get back in. David got smart and put a lock on the bottom of the door.

Ruth drove out to the pens where the calves were being sorted and were getting a wellness check and tagged. Her pretty ponytail was waving in the air and David's face lit up. She just started to do this. Usually, it was Juaquin who brought lunch but Ruth was feeling so well that she started to go out to the cowboys. She would hangout for a bit afterwards and try to help. Mostly, she would make David laugh but he was very happy that she tried. She retired from teaching when she was sick and seemed to take a new enjoyment in getting involved at the ranch. The other day, she mucked out the barn and brought in new hay all by herself. It smelled so good in the barn and David and the other guys were so happy to not have to do it themselves. He went in the house for dinner and caught her asleep at the kitchen table. He woke her up to eat then sent her to bed. Her strength was coming back, but he wished she wouldn't overdo it.

Today, she brought lunch and sat in the Jeep to watch the work. David had left Old Dan standing by the Jeep and didn't notice he had wandered off. David had trained all of his horses to stay close to him when they weren't tied up. He started to look for his big brown horse when he heard his wife laughing. She was pointing to a group of cattle that had not been worked yet. There was Old Dan, cutting out the calves and herding them into the pens. He had no rider. He just had on the saddle. David and Ruth watched him and were amazed. Soon, all the cowboys were watching as the big horse outmaneuvered the calves trying to hide behind their mothers and gently guided them into the pen. He was careful not to upset either the calf or the mother and his fluid motions were like a dance. Ruth reached into the glovebox, took out her old camera, and snapped a couple of pictures. She told David that she thought the horse could actually win a few competitions and asked him to take him to the cutting horse competition in town in two weeks. She would love to go to the rodeo arena again.

David decided to ride back with Ruth. Lunch was great and even though they were busy with calves, he wanted to spend some time with his pretty wife. He didn't care for the Jeep much, so he rode Old Dan next to her. They stopped on the way at the top of the hill with the cottonwood tree. They sat on the bench and enjoyed the view of the Pikes Peak. It was early in the summer and the air smelled like prairie grass and wild flowers. It had a sweet and lazy smell. It started out as a sunny day but as they sat and looked west, they could see the dark rainclouds forming in the mountains. In about an hour, they would get rain. Colorado summer rains didn't last long. They were short and hardly made the ground wet. Ruth loved the smell of the ranch after these rains. She would sit on the porch for hours afterwards and just sniff the smell right out of the air. The dirt road would get just enough rain to create that just-washed smell and it was one of her favorite times. David had a funny surprise for her that day. When they stood up to go, he reached up onto a branch of the old cottonwood and pulled down a swing. He had found a piece of wood his father had started to carve for a tabletop and decided to try to finish it. It was a scene of Pikes Peak and was perfect for the swing. He varnished the wood, drilled holes for the ropes, and hung it on the tree, hoping for a good time to show his wife. Ruth was delighted and sat down. It was the right height and David started to push her. She had the giggles at first like a schoolgirl but soon started to enjoy the rhythmic swinging. The sound of not-so-far-away thunder snapped them both out of the relaxing swinging and they left. Ruth drove the Jeep as fast as she could towards the barn and David had Old Dan at a full gallop. It was quite a sight, the cowboy racing the Jeep home. They both got to the barn as the first drops hit. It was a wonderful day for both of them and that day, Ruth knew that she would never leave this beautiful ranch again.

Saturday was the competition. Old Dan was more than ready. He was beautiful in the arena. David hardly had to touch him to guide him. Ruth was standing by the fence with Juaquin. She had just bought David a new Stetson to wear today and he looked handsome and at ease on his horse. They didn't win first prize but fourth wasn't bad for the first one. On the way home, they all talked about the summer and going to competitions. Old Dan had carrots and apples when he got home and when the day was done and dinner was over, everyone went to the porch to enjoy the sunset. Old Dan came over with Rosie. None of the other horses had the run of the ranch but these two horses were family. David missed rodeo and Old Dan gave him a way to compete and all of his friends turned out to watch. It was a good time. There were more cutting horse events on the rest of the summer and everyone had a lot of fun. Sometimes, as David was driving home with his wife asleep next to him and Juaquin in the back with the horse trailer behind him, he let his mind wander. The night sky was always beautiful in Colorado and for a little while, he forgot about the war he fought. He forgot about losing his parents tragically and even losing his wife for a while. He had Ironwood, Ruth, his special horses, and his friend. He would turn on the radio, put in an old Chris LeDoux tape, and sing along. Ruth would rouse a little and smile before she would rest her head on her husband's shoulder then go back to sleep as they rode home in the night.

Spring came and there was a record number of calves born each week. A mountain lion was seen several times poking around and was even in the canyon, so the calves and mothers were moved to pens closer to the barn where someone could keep a close eye on them. A few ranchers lost calves to the mountain lion, so extra caution was taken.

The weather was warming up finally and fencing had to be done. The storms and tumbleweeds were hard on the fences that year. David, Juaquin, and two other hands were out fencing. The younger ones were up on the mesa and would be there for at least a day and a half. Juaquin was working closer to the cattle and the roads and David took the short stretch to the south. He wanted to be at home that night. Fencing made him a little too tired and a hot shower and hot meal always made him feel better. When he reached the south fence, he saw a lot of problems. The tumbleweeds broke a lot of barbed wire, sometimes leaving three or four whole sections open. Juaquin had already been there with rolls of wire, fence poles, and post driver.

The old wire had to be gathered up and taken in too. A horse or cow could get tangled in wire they couldn't see, so he left empty spools too. He and the other hands would come gather it all up in the Jeep but David loved going out on the horse. He always said it's not ranching if it's not on horseback. Juaquin didn't always feel that way. He liked bumping around in the old Jeep.

That morning, David packed up his horse and headed out, but first made sure he had his 30-30 rifle and some bullets. It was an old model 94 Winchester he got from his father, who told him more than once to take it with him. Rattlesnakes and mountain lions were bad news on a ranch as big as Ironwood. David heard about the lion and would take him out if he caught him near any of his cattle. As he rode towards the south pasture, he noticed there were some bare patches in the grass. Something was laying down in the grass and the spots were too small for a cow or even a calf. David stopped at one of the spots and got off his horse. He kicked the grass aside and caught his breath when he saw under the grass a clear mountain lion print. The predator was on his ranch.

The ride to the first repair was uneventful. David would cut and roll up any old wire on the ground so his horse wouldn't get tangled up in it. Juaquin would come pick it all up later. David was lucky that Old Dan could be left standing away from the wire and wouldn't move until he was told to. When it was all clear, he would go stand next to David until the repair was finished and they would go to the next section. The first two repairs were simple and took no time at all. The third repair took out four sections. David was feeling a little uneasy about it then. He had a quick lunch and rested in the shade of an old cottonwood tree. He then took his dad's old Winchester out of the scabbard on his saddle and made sure it was loaded. He walked to the first section and leaned the rifle against the fencepost and started to cut away the wires and rolled them up. He decided to do the same at all four sections before going back to replace them. The posts were in good shape so the cleanup didn't take much time. When he got to the last section, he stopped for a minute. The hairs on the back of his neck stood up. He had a terrible feeling that someone was watching him. He looked at Old Dan who seemed relaxed. David finished the cleanup and was about to start replacing wire when he had that feeling again. This time, he looked at Old Dan. The big horse was rocking back and forth and then putting his nose in the air as if to smell something. David heard a low growl and then saw the mountain lion. He was very big coming out of the grass. He jumped up and down and yelled at the cat to try to scare him. The lion would stop for a split second and then start slowly advancing on the rancher. David would back up towards a fencepost and then stop to yell at the cat again. Old Dan was very agitated but David told him to stay where he was at. He didn't want his horse to be attacked especially with the heavy saddle that would slow him down.

He got closer to the fencepost and reached for his rifle, but then his blood ran cold.

He saw it leaning five fenceposts away. He had forgotten to move it as he moved along the fence line.

As he turned to run towards the rifle, the big cat was on him and knocked him to the ground. David had wire cutters in his hand and gloves on and was trying to knock the lion off. He could smell the hot rancid breath of the lion and he noticed how powerful and solidly muscular it was. He could see scars on the legs of the lion and even noticed how big and strong its paws were. He could see the sharp claws and he was afraid. He fought to keep the cat away from his neck and face.

David got up and started to move and the cat struck again, this time, tearing his jeans and into his skin with his claws. He was on the ground on his back kicking at the cat. He had his torn arms over his face to protect himself from the attack and finally landed a mighty kick that sent the lion several feet away. He could see the cat about halfway between him and Old Dan. The big horse wasted no time jumping towards the cat and with his teeth and jaws, he clamped down on the scruff of the lion's neck and flicked him like a rag doll a good three feet to land in a ball at David's feet. He had blood in his eyes that had dripped off the huge gashes in his forearms and couldn't clear his vision fast enough. He was afraid the cat would strike out at him when Old Dan reared up and came down full force on the lion's middle with both hooves, followed by several more until the lion was still. The horse was bigger than most and stronger too. His hooves were sharp and large and were like sledgehammers coming down again and again on the big cat. David tried to stand, but his left leg wouldn't support him. Old Dan came over and stood between David and the now dead cat as if to protect him. David noticed a large bleeding gash in Old Dan's right front leg and even though it was bleeding and was hard for him to stand on, the horse stayed with him.

He started to crawl towards the rifle with the horse so close to him. At one point, David stopped and took off his shirt. He spoke to Old Dan and, after a lot of coaxing, got the horse to come close to him. He was barely able to reach up and wrap his shirt around the horse's wound and tie it tight. The crawl to the fencepost with the rifle seemed to take forever. Several times, he had to just sit and wait for the pain in his own leg to subside. The horse waited and continued to stand between him and the dead cat. David was afraid there was another, perhaps a mate around, and kept looking over his own shoulder.

He finally got to the post with the gun. He wanted to shoot the lion to make sure he was dead but was afraid the shot would maybe attract the mate.

He leaned up against the fence and spoke softly to the lame horse. He knew Old Dan couldn't take himself home without help and would never be able to carry David. He would try if he could. He sat and promised Old Dan they would get home.

Carefully, David lifted the rifle and fired three rounds into the air in rapid succession. He waited a minute and shot three more.

He was now out of ammunition and he felt that he and Old Dan would surely die if help didn't arrive soon. He knew that Juaquin was out and headed his way to get the wire from the repairs. He hoped he would hear the shots...three shots in succession which was his signal for help.

It was only about fifteen minutes until he heard the Jeep. He knew it was Juaquin. David let his eyes close for a little bit to rest. When he opened his eyes, his old friend was holding his head and offering him a drink of water. Juaquin would have asked what happened, but he saw what was left of the lion. He had a rifle in his hand and was looking for another. He had to figure out a way to get David into the Jeep and find a way to protect Old Dan until he could get back with a trailer. Old Dan was hurt and couldn't take another step. After wrapping up David's leg and arm with gauze from a first aid kit he carried in the Jeep, he gently lifted his friend up and leaned him up on the fencepost. He wrapped David's arm around his shoulders and helped him onto the seat. He then checked on the injured horse and gave him water. There wasn't much he could do but get to the house and back as fast as he could. He had a tear in his eye as he consoled the horse and promised him he would be back. Then he carefully drove as fast as he could back to the ranch house. The other hands were just getting in when Juaquin tore into the yard with the horn blazing. There was a mad scramble to carefully lift their boss out of the Jeep and take him inside. Ruth ran outside when she heard the horn blaring and saw her husband barely conscious. Juaquin told her to get the doctor and ambulance and to call the vet. Luckily, he lived on the next ranch and could be there fast. As soon as he knew his best friend was safe, Juaquin ran to the pickup. He had moved a couple of calves that morning and had not taken the horse trailer off the truck. Normally, David would have scolded him for not taking it off but for once, he was glad he didn't. Time was not on his side and he needed to get back to Old Dan. As he drove up to the fencing site, he didn't know what to expect. When he got there, he was so happy to see that the horse was still standing there. He embraced Old Dan and gently removed his saddle and threw it in the back of the truck. Old Dan couldn't put much weight on his leg and was hesitant to get into the trailer. Juaquin held the face of the horse and slowly and gingerly led him in. Then he drove just as carefully to take the horse home as he did with David. The place was lit up when he arrived and all hands pitched in to help the horse out of the trailer. The vet was working on Old Dan before anyone could get out of his stall. It was a nasty cut on his leg and would take the whole night before they would know if they could save Old Dan.

Juaquin ran to the house to see David. The doctor and paramedics were working on stitching up his forearm and left leg. Luckily, the major blood vessels were missed but there was muscle damage. David was laying on his father's handmade kitchen table. He refused to go to the hospital until he knew how his horse was. Ruth was bringing in clean towels and boiling water to wash his wounds. She ran to hug Juaquin for saving her husband's life. She had been so brave and had not cried until her hero walked into the room. He would never know how much he meant to her and her family. When he was stitched up and in pajamas, Juaquin and the doctor put David to bed. He struggled a bit because he wanted to see Old Dan. Ruth promised him if he would rest, she would go to the barn and would wake him with any news. She and Juaquin walked to the barn where they would watch over the favored horse until morning.

It was three days before David was able to walk with crutches. Right after breakfast, he had Ruth help him to the Jeep. She and Juaquin took turns with Old Dan. The vet was there constantly with the big horse. David wanted to see Old Dan but the doctor and Ruth made him stay in bed and rest. It seemed she was constantly feeding him and finally, after much begging, she agreed to take him to the barn. The doors were wide open and a couple of the hands were cleaning out the stalls and they stepped aside as Ruth drove the Jeep inside right up to Old Dan's stall. She couldn't park too close because Rosie was standing just outside. Ruth explained that Rosie rarely left Old Dan. She just stood there and worried. She got out of the Jeep and fed carrots to Rosie and helped David out. Juaquin was in the stall with Old Dan. He was in a harness to help him to stand and gently move without putting weight on his injured leg. His head was down and he barely moved. Then he heard David say, "Hi, old buddy." The horse's ears perked right up and with great effort, he lifted his massive head. David went to hug his old friend. He didn't want to hurt him and was very careful. This horse saved his life and he wanted him to know how grateful he was. As David stroked his horse's velvety face, he told Ruth and Juaquin what had happened. Juaquin had gone out to get the wire and finish the fence early that morning and was going to bring back the lion. But it was no longer there. All that was left was a large bloodstain in the grass. The grass was stomped down by Old Dan's hooves and there were no drag marks. Juaquin didn't go alone so one of the hands stood watch with a rifle while the little bit of work that was left got finished. Juaquin didn't think they would see another big cat on the ranch again.

As he was visiting his horse, the veterinarian showed up. He explained that Old Dan had torn muscles and a torn ligament. He stitched him up and was so glad the horse didn't have to be put down. With lots of therapy and care of the wound, the big horse would recover. The bad news was that leg would never support a saddle, let alone a person. He knew how much David cared for his horse. He never heard such a heroic story, so he did everything he could do to save his life.

A few weeks passed, David was walking with one crutch and could make it to the barn by himself. Old Dan was gingerly stepping on his bad leg. It was starting to heal and there would be a very bad scar. Today he was going to go outside. Juaquin walked him to the door with Ruth. They tried to coax him out, but he would pull back when he got to the door out to the pen. He seemed scared and wouldn't be enticed out into the sunshine by Ruth's yummy carrots. They were about to take him back to his stall when Old Dan spotted something at the other end of the pens. Ruth and Juaquin looked and could only see Rosie. Then David carefully stepped around her and Old Dan started to walk towards him. He still had a limp, but nothing could stop him from being with David. Ruth handed her husband the big carrots and left him alone with his horse. She sat on the fence with Juaquin and watched the two walk. It was quite a sight. They both limped and struggled but they made it around the pen. The pain and exhaustion were clear on both of their faces, so Ruth shouted at them to go inside. The whole time they were walking, Rosie was behind them. She walked very slowly with her head down, as if to catch either one should they fall. At first, it made Juaquin nervous but he saw that she paced herself so as not to get too close. Every day for the rest of the summer, David would go do physical therapy with Old Dan. His doctor was impressed at his improvement. By the end of summer, they were able to walk for hours. The entire time, Rosie would follow them. Early September, Old Dan was in the pen by himself. Rosie walked to him and gently pushed him towards the gate. When they got to the gate, she reached over and pushed the latch aside and opened it. She held the gate open and waited for Old Dan. Then she reached down and took the short lead rope Juaquin walked her with into her mouth then walked to the house with the big velvety horse behind her. She pulled him up onto the porch and waited at the Dutch door for Ruth. Ruth was in the kitchen making her peanut butter cookies and when she saw Rosie, she jumped. Rosie hadn't been to the house in a long time. Ruth called out to David that Rosie was there and went to the door with a handful of cookies. Her husband who used a cane that time limped to the door right behind her. The cookies were for him and he didn't want Rosie to eat them all. They opened the rest of the door and were both surprised to see the porch full of two horses. Ruth laughed at Rosie and gave them both a cookie and an apple. She led them off the porch and watched as the smaller horse took the lead rope again and led Old Dan back to the barn. David laughed too; he had not laughed like that since the day of the attack. He never thought Old Dan would leave the pens, the mountain lion scared him. But Rosie knew just what to do.

Every day, there was a visit from the two horses. David could lead Old Dan around, but his ears twitched and he jumped every time he heard a noise. David was a little jumpy too and sometimes carried his rifle with him. But when Rosie had the big horse's lead rope, he was very calm and followed her everywhere. It wasn't all good, though. Rosie wasn't a good influence on Old Dan.

One day, she managed to get the kitchen door open and both were inside knocking things over and banging the furniture. Ruth's favorite cup got broken and so did the cookie jar. It took the bewildered couple fifteen minutes to get them turned around and back out the door. The whole time, Rosie held onto Dan.

Ruth had a short fence around her garden. She had pretty fall flowers growing alongside tomatoes and carrots, and she even tried her hand at hot peppers for Juaquin. Rosie brought her companion and knocked a whole section of fence over to get in the garden. The first thing to go was the pretty yellow and orange flowers. She would pull them up and shared them with Dan. The tomatoes were next. They were big and ripe and they were gone in no time: the whole plant. A few carrots were pulled up before Rosie found the Jalapeno pepper plants. No one would have heard them until Old Dan started to react to the hot pepper. He stomped, yelped, coughed, and started to look for water. Ruth came out and led both of them to the trough to get some water. She would have been angry except the look on their faces made her laugh and the longer they stayed at the trough, the funnier it got. The two horses were still there when it got dark and Juaquin had to lead them back to the barn.

The horses stayed out of the garden and kitchen for a while. Everyone thought the hot peppers taught them a lesson.

It was early October when Ruth decided to wash all the sheets and David's mother's quilts. It was hot and sunny out and she raised the clothesline to hang the sheets to dry and whiten in the bright fall sunlight. Everything would smell so fresh when it was time to make the beds. The first round of sheets was on the line and Ruth was starting to hang the quilts. She had three on the line and went inside to get more. Rosie took Dan out of the barn for his walk. He was doing so much better but still refused to leave by himself. Along the back fence was some rhubarb and they stopped to munch on the still tender sweet stalks. The gate to the garden was closed, but the horses were free to wander in the yard. As they were standing in the yard, a bunny found its way out of the garden. Ruth was losing her garden to horses and rabbits this year. The bunny startled Old Dan and he tried to get away, but Rosie still had the lead rope in her mouth. She tried to keep up with Old Dan, but the clothesline pole was in the way. Both of them got tangled in the sheets and quilts. Clothespins were flying and sheets and quilts were on the horses and on the ground. Rosie finally let go of Old Dan's rope and they stopped struggling. Ruth heard the commotion and came out of the house to see the clothesline cleared and the two horses covered with laundry from face to tail. David followed her out of the house and watched her peel the laundry off of the two guilty-looking animals. He was laughing so hard at the two of them that he had to sit down.

After the laundry was back in the basket, Ruth pet both horses to let them know they weren't in trouble and sent them back towards the pen. That time, Rosie didn't have to take Old Dan's rope. He wasn't shaking and nervous anymore. David stood up, scratched his head, and helped his wife redo the wash.

Chapter 9

David and Old Dan healed. The big horse couldn't wear a saddle anymore or take a rider but that was okay. He was getting old and was more like a family friend. David was in his sixties then and was riding Rosie. She wasn't the good cutting horse that Rusty and Old Dan were, but she was the most surefooted and smooth ride David ever had. He had to get her a new saddle. It was plain but fit her very well and she never had a sore spot after a long day. He didn't ride her very much but when he did, it was just for pleasure. Ruth rode her too and she was so gentle with his wife that she never complained of being sore and tired. Ruth was funny when she went for a ride. She had a nice straw hat but somehow the edges were nibbled away by Rosie. His wife kept the hat and felt that each bite was Rosie's way of showing love. There were two odd things about Rosie. One was how much she loved to ride the hoodoos in the canyon. None of the horses liked it in there but she did. The multicolored cliffs and caves were hers to explore. David liked riding in the canyon. He would ride out there with Ruth and Rusty but could tell that Rusty didn't like going in there. Sunsets in the canyons were pretty and David fell in love with Ruth there. The other odd thing was they would saddle up and ride a little way and Rosie would start to talk with him. Not people talk, just nod her head and say "hmmm" and "oh" to let him know she was listening. If he didn't talk, she would go for miles making the worst whinny sounds till he would talk. David loved to take his notebook and lunch for these rides. Rosie would stand perfectly still while he would brace his notebook on the saddle horn and write. She brought out the best in him and sometimes their conversations made him fill the whole notebook.

David would have good days and bad days. Some days, he just stayed home. The wound from the mountain lion was sore at times. Those were the days he would spend with Old Dan. He would wash him, brush him, rub liniment on the horse's leg, and take him out for a walk. Sometimes, he would take him to the bench on the hill to write and watch the storms coming from the west. Juaquin was running the ranch with several foremen now and David would run into town for supplies with Ruth, stop at the post office for some town gossip, and lunch at Roosters. Some days, he would dress up and take his still pretty wife out for a nice lunch and movie in Colorado Springs.

He still went to auctions, but it was more modern these days. His friends seemed older to him now, but it was always good to see them. On his good days, he would ride out with Rosie to help with cattle sorting or the well calf operations. Even though Juaquin was several years older than he was, he had a way with horses still and it was always fun to watch him cutting calves. Ironwood was a much bigger ranch now. He added onto the ranch house and built a nice one for Juaquin. The barn was torn down and replaced by a steel building. That way, he could walk Old Dan in the wintertime too. There was a new bunkhouse and he had several full-time hands who lived on the ranch, and there was room for the seasonal ones. Juaquin always had a way of making sure there was plenty of help. Ruth and David's mother had planted trees by the front gate and they had grown so tall that they towered over the hand-carved entrance. He was glad he chose to keep Ironwood. He and Rosie would ride every inch of it and enjoy it all. Of course, he now carried a handgun and a rifle and watched for a mountain lion. Truthfully, nobody had seen one on the ranch or even the neighbor's ranches since the attack. No one quite knew what happened to the big cat's body. Most speculated that it was taken by his mate, but there were no prints in the grass and no drag marks. It was as if he was scooped up from that spot and made to disappear.

Winter came, David and Ruth finally got a DVD player and would pick up movies when they were in town. If they weren't inside the nice, warm barn with the horses and occasionally handfeeding a calf, they were snuggled up by the fire watching movies. The snows started early that year and there were days when the storm would go on and on. The wind howled outside and made the hairs on their arms stand up. On those days, David would really feel his age. Lately, he would have numbness in his arms or feel a tightening in his chest. Nothing worked right and he would get dizzy when he got up too fast. These were small issues to him and he chose to ignore them. He was never sick, and the most he was around the doctors was when Ruth was so sick or when he was injured. He had made peace with his age and was glad he had his wife to compare aches and pains with. She was still vibrant and loved her jeans, Ropers, and signature blonde ponytail. Her blue eyes still sparkled when he entered the room and he was so happy to have her in his life. She still made him laugh and made the bed warm at night too. Her relationship with Rosie made them even closer. The pretty and mischievous horse was like a child they never had. They both regretted not having children, but life was so busy on the ranch that they had no time to think much about it.

Spring came, David wasn't feeling too much better but it was calving season and even though he wasn't up to the physical taxing job of helping, he would saddle Rosie up and take his rifle to watch for predators. That was what attracted the lion to the ranch and led to the attack. He would just ride and stand watch. He didn't go out in the bad weather; his leg would get stiff and it was hard to sit in a saddle all day.

David and Juaquin would watch the news to check on the weather every day. One day, the forecast was for a front to come up from New Mexico and curl up against the Front Range and stay there for days. The snow would vary from light to intense but was not predicted to stop for at least a week. Most of the time, the snows didn't make it past the continental divide and the prairies only got a little snow followed up by days of sunshine. That year was different. It was cold and windy and the snow had piled up against the fences. There was going to be a lot of repairs this summer. The decision was made to move most of the cattle closer then put the mothers and calves in the pens and make sure they had a lot of hay. Preparations were made and the cattle were moving. They were out in different parts of the ranch so it would be a slow process. David hoped they would all be in and accounted for before the storm was upon them. Rosie was good at finding calves and he was ready at a moment's notice to go get any strays, but he prayed that that wouldn't happen. Sometimes he would find them too late.

The first snows started to roll in and Juaquin came in with a tally sheet to compare to the tag numbers. He and the other hands had been out rounding up calves and moms for two days and they were thinking they had them all. They worked out there day and night and the cook had to bring them food. Everyone was exhausted and still had to brush and bed the horses, secure the barn, and put out hay and feed for the cattle. They were all tired and dirty and wanting a warm bed. While they were winding the preparations for the storm down, Juaquin went in to check the books. He sat down for dinner with Ruth and David. Ruth noticed how tired he looked and noticed his age. She was amazed at how long the old cowboys in her life would work. After dinner, they brought out the ledger books and started to check off the tag numbers of that year's calves. Even though Juaquin had covered the whole ranch and was meticulous about checking tags, there were two missing. He thought it was his tired old eyes so he asked Ruth to doublecheck. Two tags were missing. Two calves were missing. Juaquin had gone out in the Jeep and looked everywhere before he came in. That could only mean one of two things: a mountain lion or a coyote got them, or they were in the canyon. If they were in the canyon, they would get lost in there. He stood up from the table and put on his Carhartt and prepared to go look again. David stopped him. He pointed out that he was tired and the Jeep only could go to the entrance. The rest had to be done on foot. He sent Juaquin home and said he and Rosie would go find the calves. The ranch hand and Ruth gave each other a concerned look, but both of them knew they could never talk him out of going. He, at least, let them talk him into waiting for morning.

Early the next morning, the snow was just starting to fall. The flakes were pretty; they swirled and had not started to stick on the ground yet. David saddled Rosie and packed extra clothes and blankets. He packed some food while telling Ruth he would be back that afternoon. That time, Ruth had a worried look on her face. It reminded him of his mother when he rode the bull. He walked back across the porch, took her chin in his hand, and tilted her face up to look him in the eyes. He promised her he would return and kissed his wife. It was the same protective and sweet kiss as their first. It always made her feel safe. She reached her arms around his neck, put her face on his chest, and said she believed him. He left in the dark on Rosie. They hadn't gone very far when the snow intensified. The ground was already covered and to make things worse, the wind kicked up and the visibility was getting bad. David wouldn't have been able to see the calves in the grass anyway, unless he rode right on top of them, so he rode directly towards the canyon. It was noon by the time they reached the entrance and the snow was at least six inches deep. It slowed the horse down. David got out a blanket and wrapped it around himself and parts of Rosie. They kept on going. They entered the canyon and the wind died down. Immediately, they heard the calves crying. There were so many spires that they found themselves wandering in and around each rock formation. They didn't want to miss them. David only hoped to find them together. The snow got deeper and deeper and soon it was up to Rosie's knees. She was so surefooted and lifted each leg carefully out of the snow. It was starting to get dark and David got out his flashlight. They rounded a large rock formation when he spotted them. They were together. The snow was almost up to their shoulders and they were crying and shivering. He got rope out to put around their necks so he could lead them to shelter. It was hard to walk in the deep snow. Rosie walked ahead of him so he could follow her tracks. She would make sounds at him as if she was talking to him and he answered her back. He kept telling her he hoped she knew what she was doing. They were going further into the canyon and he was getting very nervous. Rosie stopped. David walked up beside her and looked around. He didn't see anything in the formations that would offer shelter from the snow. As he stood there puzzled, Rosie pushed him to her left. He still couldn't see anything. She kept pushing his back and as he brushed up onto a spire, he could see it. He never saw the cave before, even when he was a boy. David quickly grabbed a shovel and cleared the cave entrance. It wasn't a big cave but it was a shelter. He pushed the calves in first and went in himself after grabbing all he could from the saddle. He had blankets, clothes, water, and food. He had some carrots and pellets for Rosie. The calves were standing in the back of the cave and had stopped shivering. David wrapped himself in blankets and had an extra for his horse. She didn't fit all the way in but he thought she would be okay in the entrance. It wasn't very big and if David fell asleep, she would keep the calves inside. It was quiet in the cave as he ate and drank. He talked to the horse who nodded and made noises back at him. He was starting to warm up and get drowsy but Rosie kept him awake by nudging his foot with her nose from time to time. David felt bad for breaking his promise to Ruth. He was afraid she would try to come get him and would get lost in the deep snow. All night, Rosie stood watch over the cave with him in it.

Dawn came and the calves were crying and restless again. It had stopped snowing. David stood up and felt that familiar ache in his chest. It must have been from sleeping on the rocks. He was getting too old for that.

He loaded everything on Rosie and pulled the calves out of the cave. Rosie would walk ahead of him and he would walk in the path in the deep snow dragging the calves. Maybe when they got out of the canyon, the snow would be blown away enough to get further. If it were one calf, he would put her on the saddle with him, but there were two and he couldn't manage both. They got to where he found the calves and turned the corner and there was Juaquin. He was never so happy to see him. He lifted one calf onto Juaquin's saddle and one onto his own and climbed on himself. They were met by more hands as they got closer to the house, and they handed the calves off to them then went home. Exhaustion set in and David barely made it into the house. Juaquin took Rosie to the barn and Ruth took care of her husband. He was shivering and she brought him warm blankets. The fireplace was blazing, yet he kept shivering. His wife brought him a steaming cup of coffee and some dinner. He couldn't pick up the mug with one hand and she had to help him. He explained to her that his hands and arms were numb and ached from lying on the cold rocks in the cave. Ruth gave him aspirin and helped him to eat before drawing him a very hot bath. The whole time she was taking care of him, he was remembering his mother doing the same after the bull injured him. He had broken a promise to her and he could see the same sad look on Ruth's face. As he was eating the hot and flavorful stew, he stopped and looked at the fire. His gaze went to the mantle and there was the bull statue he gave his mother. He felt so bad that he grabbed his wife's hand and held it. He told her how very sorry he was and how he worried all night that she would get a horse and come looking for him. The corner of Ruth's eyes lit up and she smiled a little and said she did. Even the horse had better sense and wouldn't budge. She kissed her husband's forehead and went to draw his bath. It would be a sleepy day for them both. No one had got any sleep the night before. The next morning, she took a large handful of carrots and apples to her girl, Rosie. As she rested her face on the nose of her busily chomping horse, she cried. She could not thank this horse enough for saving his life. As she walked out of the stall to return to the house, she stopped and reached for her straw hat hanging on a peg. She handed it to Rosie, who promptly ate it.

David felt better in a few days and didn't see a need to go to a doctor, no matter how much his wife asked him to. He spent more time at the house and on sunny days on the porch.

Summer came and Rosie and David spent time together. Ruth came along on some of the rides and made him fall in love with her all over again. Some days, Old Dan would come along but David noticed that he tired easily and would turn around to go back to the barn. The velvety big horse wasn't the only one to tire easily these days. David and Rosie wouldn't go near the fences and just spent time going for mail or riding the pastures and just enjoying the smells and views. Ironwood was a big ranch and they kept very busy just enjoying the rides. David had his notebook with him and some days just wrote his memories in the books. Sometimes he was too tired or achy to even saddle Rosie. He contributed it to old age and the lion attack. Rosie would hangout by the garden but that year, Ruth put a bigger fence and a better latch on the gate. She wanted tomatoes that year and that horse needed to stay out. The sad look on Rosie's face told Ruth how she felt about it. If she stayed by the garden too many days in a row, Ruth would put on her jeans and Ropers and go take her for a ride. That summer, David made Ruth learn to shoot both the rifle and pistol. She always had one with her on her rides. She enjoyed her time with Rosie. They would go to the tree and bench and check out Pikes Peak. Sometimes, they would just ride to the last stock tank to the north. The view of the whole valley was so pretty there and Ruth would always take a camera. Sometimes she would just ride and talk. There was no better listener than that red horse. Ruth was concerned about how tired David was and wanted to do something with him that they never did before; take a vacation. It was hard to imagine a place more beautiful or restful than Ironwood Ranch.

Summer turned to fall. It was one of the most beautiful ones on the ranch. The leaves turned various shades of red, orange, and yellow. It started with the stand of aspens in the front yard, and then the cottonwoods and elms turned. Most years, they just turned brown and fell, but the days were long and warm still and nights were cool and crisp. They had some late summer rain and it made the leaves hang on tight. David and Ruth still enjoyed the walk up the hill to watch the sun set behind Pikes Peak from the bench and the leaves made a nice crunching sound under their feet. These days, David walked a little slower, but Ruth found the slow trip relaxing. Sometimes Old Dan was at the top of the hill waiting for them and the three would enjoy the sunset together. Old Dan would get a lot of petting which seemed to perk him right up and sometimes, he would actually trot back to the barn. As the autumn wore on, the cool air was there all day and the wind sometimes blew. Usually, the day after a windy day was warm. It was a good thing too. The tumbleweeds were abundant this year and it seemed that Ironwood got more than its share of them. They would pile up against the fences and when it was windy, the weight of them would break some wires.

David made a mental note that the next time there would be several warm days in a row, he would go out to clear them away and repair the damage before it became too much.

A few weeks later, the weather held up. It was unseasonably warm for days and promised more such days. Juaquin was out on the Jeep pulling tumbleweeds and David decided to give Rosie a try and fix some fences too. He was at the top of the hill, letting his thoughts and memories catch up with him. It was a good life. The sun was starting to shine on

Pikes Peak. David never got tired looking at this mountain. The dried leaves and hay made the air smell good and the birds were starting to wake up and sing. From the meadowlarks in the tall grass to the mourning doves cooing in the tree, they all sounded like a symphony to him. David was tired but happy. He had a great life at Ironwood. He had a beautiful wife that he lost and brought home. He had parents that loved him and left him a legacy. David thought about the three horses that he loved in his life and how all of them have saved his life. He remembered his friends and the town. The cowboy was getting older and tired and was in his winter trail; the time when things slow down and younger people run the ranch, and the time when a ride on his horse was no longer work but pleasure. He was dressed nice today and was in no hurry to get to the fence. Today was the day to give thanks and to ride tall in his saddle once more.

The ride to the fence was very nice. Sunrise on a prairie was golden and the breeze made a nice melody in the grasses. Today, he could smell the sage that grew along the fences. He only had a few areas to clear before lunch, but stopped when he saw a spot at the top of the rise that had a big tangle of tumbleweeds. Rosie found the little creek bed that wove in and out of the fence and stopped to have a drink and chew on the grass. David sat up against a small tree with his rifle and pistol at his side and ate his lunch. He started to write in the notebook when he stopped to take out a bag filled with his wife's famous peanut butter cookies. Rosie must have smelled her favorite treat because in no time, she was next to him trying to get his cookies. David was laughing at her antics. She was a funny horse. Not as talented as Old Dan, but she kept him entertained. Lunch was over and David gave up on defending the cookies and let the horse have one. The other was tucked into his shirt pocket for later. He went to the fence with his gun and started to untangle the weeds. The rifle was never more than a foot or two away from his hand. The tangled mess was so bad that David had to cut them apart with the wire cutters. He was making very good progress when he felt a tightening in his chest. Nothing to be concerned about, wrestling with tumbleweeds was hard work and he was starting to sweat and get a little winded. The tightness in his chest was making him tired, sleepy, and short of breath. David decided to sit in the shade close by where he was working. Just for a short break, a little water, and a cool-down. Rosie came and stood next to him. She stood very still and just watched him. He wanted to be comfortable and give Rosie a break, so he wrestled the saddle off her and spread her blanket on the ground. He leaned up against the saddle and rested.

David took his book and short pencil out of his pocket and got out his father's old pocketknife. After sharpening his pencil to a fine point, he started to write. Today was the day he wanted to talk to God. He dressed up in his best hat and boots. It was important to him to give thanks today. It was cool in the shade and he started to talk. Life had been full of ups and downs. Sometimes, it was hard to see what direction to go in and David's mother taught him to listen to God and he will find a way. He listened to the breeze in the trees, the birds, and the sounds of the cattle. To him, God was everywhere and he just needed to look and listen. David gave thanks for his mother who provided a spiritual guidance and gave him the notebooks. They got him through some very hard times. He gave thanks for his father who showed him to work hard and love the ranch and especially his love for his horses. He gave thanks for his beloved Ruth and gave thanks for finding her again and saving her life. It seemed like God smoothed over the years she was gone and made the memories a blessed blur. David gave thanks for Juaquin, his friend and mentor. His sense of humor was the glue that held the ranch together. He also gave thanks for Rusty, his first horse. There was no better friend. There was thanks for Old Dan, the biggest and strongest horse who would offer up his life for David. And there was Rosie; she helped Ruth to get well and her antics were just what they needed. He also gave thanks for the hard times in his life. He confessed that there were times that his faith was shaken to the core. When he was in Viet Nam and the way he felt when he came back. When his parents died in the horrible storm and he turned his back on Ironwood. But each time, a hand was held out to him to guide him back.

A ray of sunshine fell on his face through the leaves of the tree. God had answered him back.

David didn't know what else to write in his book. He was looking at the entries and as he felt his eyes getting heavy, he was finally comfortable and was thinking it wouldn't be so bad to take a little nap.

He rested his head against his saddle.

It was a sight: the cowboy leaning on his saddle, his head bowed as if in prayer, his hand holding the old notebook, and the stubby pencil falling from his hand. David fell into a sleep he will never awake from, at least on this earth. Rosie was standing beside him, lazily grazing on the short green grass at her feet. Then she started with her head tilted toward the cowboy. She knew he was gone, but obediently, she would stay by his side until they were found later.

Chapter 10

Two days ago, there was a relentless wind from the east. The tumbleweeds seemed to roll in on it. They piled up on the barbed wire fences but seemed to want to roll right by the ranch house and barn. But yesterday was calm and unusually warm. The air was scrubbed clean by the wind and the sunrise was a pretty orange and silver. The funeral was very nice; the church was packed and overflowed. The neighbors came. The men wore their nice western slacks, white shirts with string ties, black Stetsons, and dress boots. The women wore pantsuits and their hair couldn't be moved by the wind. There were so many cars on Highway 24 that they stretched out from one end of town to the other and beyond. The service lasted an extra hour so that everyone who wanted to tell their story about David could do so. There was so much. His school friends and rodeo buddies. They spoke of his famous ride on the bull that couldn't be ridden. Ruth knew some of these stories, but a lot of them were a surprise. They made her smile and cry, and laugh and cry some more. Her admiration for her husband grew ten times that morning.

The air was balmy and calm when they followed the simple yet elegant pine coffin out to the horse-drawn wagon. It was a tradition in David's family to walk the two blocks behind the wagon with the flag-draped coffin to the cemetery.

The Veterans Administration sent out a detail to give David military honors. He didn't want to be buried at Fort Logan in Denver. It was a beautiful veteran cemetery, but David had a plot in the small local cemetery next to his parents. The men in uniform lifted him from the wagon with care and carried him the short distance through the gates and to his family plot. His parents were there and on his other side was room for Ruth.

She appreciated the respect and honor of the 21-gun salute, the bugle playing taps, and the presentation of the flag to her.

They had a beautiful lunch at the church basement. The flowers were brought down and gave the room a sweet outdoor smell. So much food was brought that after the reception, the church ladies packed some of it up for her to take home.

Today was hard to face. Getting back to normal was hard for Ruth. David was gone for a week. The new foreman and his wife were moving to the ranch today. He would take care of the cattle and life on the ranch would go on. Juaquin was still there but moved into the house so the bunkhouse could be remodeled for them.

Ruth had grown to love this land. The simple life made her healthier and happier than she thought would be possible. Now, she would pass that legacy onto another young couple. She watched the sun come up through her big bedroom window. It wasn't like her to be in bed after sunrise. Ruth slowly got out of bed and told herself to start there. It will get easier, just start. David filled her head and she found that if she kept him there and didn't let him go to her heart, she wouldn't cry. She could do it. She wanted to make him proud. Ruth got out of bed and bent over to pick up her nice black dress. She had worn it to dances, church, and funerals, but yesterday when it hit the floor, she knew she would never wear it again.

She wandered into the bathroom to shower and dropped it into the trash. After the long hot shower, she put her long blonde hair into its usual ponytail. After all these years, her sun-bleached hair still didn't have gray in it. On went the worn jeans and Ropers and Carhartt jacket. Coffee was ready like it always was and out to the porch she went. Rosie was already there to get a carrot and have her beautiful face rubbed. Ruth hadn't ridden Rosie since she found her watching over David with no saddle. Today was going to be different. Today she would ride the lonely and faithful horse. She would brush her down and sing to her like David did. "Red River Valley." She would do the chores in the barn and would go out to talk to Old Dan in the corral. It seemed that since Rosie came back, Old Dan has kept his head down and not eaten much. David would not have liked that, so Ruth was going to cheer the old horse up.

She went back into the kitchen to get another cup of coffee and saw the notebook still on the table in the kitchen. His perfect handwriting was on the small papers, and he told her where he was and how beautiful the day was. Looking back to the day he died, the day he went out to fence with his nice boots and hat, Ruth got a feeling something wasn't right. He spent too long over a cup of coffee and his kiss felt different. When early afternoon came and she didn't see her husband and horse, she got a very sick feeling something was wrong. She had to get to David. Juaquin and her took the Jeep and went to get her husband. He was several miles away by a broken, tumbleweed-tangled mess of a fence. The saddle was on the ground and David was leaning on it with his head down. His Stetson covered his face and it looked like he was just taking a nap. She knew he was gone. The cowboy had his notebook, pencil, and pocketknife on one side on him and some wire cutters on the other side. They gathered David up carefully and put him on the backseat of the old Jeep. Juaquin tried to put the saddle carefully back on Rosie but she would step away every time. Finally, Ruth lifted the heavy saddle and Rosie bent down as if to help her. Ruth got into the back of the Jeep and held her husband, cradling his head in her lap as they slowly moved for home. Rosie didn't need to be tied to the car, she followed with her head down out of respect for her cowboy.

So here Ruth was, with the notebook in her hand. She put her cup down and started to read. It wasn't about the fence or the ranch. It was about how beautiful the stars were that early morning and how much he loved her. Her eyes started to water as he apologized for leaving her like this but thought it was the best way to go. Ruth put the paper on the table and walked to their bedroom closet. On the shelf was his Stetson and the wooden box. She reached up and touched the Stetson lovingly and grabbed the box and took it into the kitchen.

She was going to just put the notes in the box, but when she opened it, it was full and there was no room. Ruth sat down with her coffee and began to read the notes. Amazingly, they were in order and David dated every single piece of paper. She used to laugh when he would put notebooks on her grocery list. They became so hard to get that she had to go to Colorado Springs to get them and stock him up. Now as she was reading, she cried, for in front of her was the story of his life. Some she knew and some she didn't. This man was a delight and a mystery. The box was full of the gold that was his life and she was so glad she was a part of it.

As she read, she thought, *He isn't gone. He is just waiting. He and Rusty. Waiting for Old Dan, Rosie, Juaquin, and me.*